CW00881699

GUARDED

HOSTAGE RESCUE TEAM SERIES

KAYLEA CROSS

GUARDED

Copyright © 2018
by Kaylea Cross

* * * * *

Cover Art & Print Formatting:
Sweet 'N Spicy Designs
Developmental edits: Deborah Nemeth
Line Edits: Joan Nichols
Digital Formatting: LK Campbell

* * * * *

This book is a work of fiction. The names, characters, places, and incidents are products of the writer's imagination or have been used fictitiously and are not to be construed as real. Any resemblance to persons, living or dead, actual events, locales or organizations is entirely coincidental.

All rights reserved. With the exception of quotes used in reviews, this book may not be reproduced or used in whole or in part by any means existing without written permission from the author.

ISBN: 978-1722044763

Dedication

For Nav, for sharing your medical expertise about maternity and newborn care with me. You are a shining light both in your family and community, and I am so grateful that there are people like you making our world a better place each day. Thank you, and shine on.

And for all you HRT fans who demanded another glimpse into Matt and Briar's life! I'm glad you asked, because I wanted to spend some time with them too, and because this story hits close to home for me :).

Happy reading!
Kaylea

Author's Note

As an author it's tough to finish up a series and let go of the cast of characters I love, so it's extra special for me when I can write new stories and hang out with them again.

This one feels really personal because it includes a lot of my own experiences both before and after I had my sons. So to every woman out there who suddenly questioned everything about her mothering skills after baby arrived—especially the ability to keep a newborn alive—this one's for you. I promise you it doesn't make you a bad person, and you're definitely not alone!

Chapter One

Stretched out on her belly on a wooded ridge overlooking the valley floor, Briar stared through her night vision riflescope at the log cabin below. The scent of the forest surrounded her, damp and earthy and fresh after a hard rain that had just eased to a light shower a few minutes ago.

"I count five heat signatures in the house," she murmured, careful not to let her voice carry.

"I'm seeing the same." Lying in supported prone position beside her, her boss Alex Rycroft studied the small screen in his hands. The image showed an infrared feed from a drone circling the area high above. "Command, can you confirm?" he asked quietly.

The answer came through their earpieces a moment later. "Affirmative. Five tangos in target location."

Even though it was damp and cold, Briar was loving every second of this. It had been too damn long since she'd been out in the field. Even longer since she'd acted as a sniper.

A health scare during an op more than a year ago was to blame. She had been hit with some kind of Taser that had triggered cardiac arrest due to an undiagnosed arrhythmia she hadn't been aware of. Since then she'd mostly been working as an analyst.

It felt good to be back in her element, though she wasn't used to having a spotter with her. Back when she'd been a secret government assassin in the Valkyrie Program, she'd always worked alone. Working with Rycroft was awesome, however. He was former SF and had more experience than anyone she'd worked with before. Tonight they were providing recon and acting as overwatch if a tactical team was called in for a direct assault on the target.

The feel of the sniper rifle in her hands soothed her and gave her a sense of calm. She was good at this. It was what she did best, actually. When she got home, she would have to hit the range with Matt and get her fix. Because after this op, her sniping days were pretty much over.

"There should be more of them," Rycroft murmured to her.

Briar never took her eyes from the scope, the cold and damp after being camped out in the rain for the past two days barely registering. Learning how to ignore physical discomfort was one of the first things that had been drilled into her in the Valkyrie Program.

That, and to never trust or rely on anyone but herself.

Reversing that ingrained programming had proven hardest for her since joining the civilian world. She still struggled with trusting people, letting them in. Sometimes it even came up with her husband, Matt, who thankfully still wanted to keep her around.

Briar focused on the cabin, analyzing it. "Think anyone's in a cellar under there maybe?" There wouldn't be a basement; the structure was too old and crudely built to have one. But an old storage cellar was a possibility.

"Maybe."

So far the five people in the cabin hadn't come back out. She did another slow sweep of the area, making sure she hadn't missed anything. This right-wing group had gained support and attention in recent months. They were reportedly planning a major attack on a soft, civilian target in NYC. Fucking hateful cowards.

A flash of movement caught her attention.

"Wait, I've got movement in the trees to the northeast." She zeroed in on it. As she watched, adjusting the scope's focus, three more figures emerged from the tree line to the right of the cabin. All men, and all dressed in tactical gear they'd probably bought at the nearest surplus store.

They didn't move like amateurs, though. They moved slowly, appeared to be alert and cautious as they scanned the area, each of them holding what looked like M4s. "Bodyguards?" she murmured.

"Could be." A pause as Rycroft switched frequencies. "Get me an overhead visual," he said to the drone pilot.

"Roger that," came the response.

"You recognize any of them?" Rycroft asked her.

"No." None of them matched the pictures she'd memorized of the group's leader and other key members. Three of who were already inside the cabin. The NSA, FBI and DHS wanted them all captured.

While Rycroft watched his screen, Briar kept her attention on the men emerging from the trees. The group's leader was supposed to be here, yet he wasn't one of the five men in the cabin. She'd watched each one arrive, and he hadn't shown. These three newcomers moved like they were disciplined and had some kind of tactical training. Not a total surprise, since many members of the group were reported to be former military.

But none of them knew she and Rycroft were up here, watching. None of them knew they were in her crosshairs, or that she could kill any one of them with a squeeze of the trigger. She had used this weapon for more than a decade. It was calibrated specifically for her frame and preferences, so perfect it was like an extension of her body.

"Someone's coming out the front door," she said.

A man stepped out onto the front porch seconds later, holding a flat object in his hands. He shook it out, reached up and attached it to something sticking out of the front wall.

A freaking Nazi flag to mark their repulsive clubhouse.

"Lovely," she muttered under her breath.

"Looks like they're rolling out the old welcome mat for someone special," Rycroft said.

The leader. He had to be either on his way, or nearby. She scanned the trees again. Why couldn't she see him? "The detail's stopped moving." The three men in front of the tree line all stood several paces apart, maintaining a secure perimeter. "Waiting for someone."

She adjusted her aim, centering her crosshairs on the middle guy. This had to be it. All the NSA's intel said Dempsey would be here tonight, to plan the upcoming attack with the other high-ranking members. Home grown terrorists, every single one of them.

"I'm alerting the team." Rycroft contacted the commander of the FBI tactical team back at the command post fifteen miles away. An FBI SWAT team. "Your boys ready to go?"

"Affirmative. Everyone's on board, helo's ready to launch."

"Might have found what we're looking for. Stand by." Then to her, "They're at a field five miles from here. Can be here in a couple minutes if we pull the trigger on this thing."

Oh, how she loved to pull the trigger on bad guys.

Briar listened with half an ear, more interested in who the guard detail was waiting for. She didn't have to wait long to find out.

More figures appeared through the dense forest of trees. Two big men. A third trailing a few steps behind them, moving without as much caution. "You seeing this?" she whispered to Rycroft.

"Trees are too thick for the drone." He picked up his spotter scope instead, located the men. "Can you ID any of the newcomers?"

"Not the first two." The third man finally came into view, and a flash of elation hit her. "It's Dempsey." There was no mistaking that bearded face.

She adjusted her grip on her weapon, snugged her right cheek against the buttstock, her index finger on the trigger guard. She centered her crosshairs over his chest and waited.

The difference was still jarring. In her former life she would already have put a bullet through him and be packing up to move out of the area as fast as she could. But the rules were different now. She could only fire under direct orders from Rycroft or if someone posed a direct threat to her or someone else on their team.

She couldn't help it if she hoped this asshole gave her a reason to fire. One less twisted human cockroach for the world to worry about.

Rycroft contacted the team commander again. "Target confirmed. Move in."

"Roger that," the commander responded. "ETA four minutes."

Briar kept careful watch as the security detail escorted Dempsey to the cabin. The guy on the porch was there to meet him. His four buddies inside came out to greet their leader with Nazi salutes.

Her lip curled in disgust. Too bad the NSA wanted these guys alive, for questioning and prosecution. She would rather end this a different way. But that was just her, because she was savage when it came to stuff like this. Luckily, Matt loved that about her.

Everything moved fast from that point. Onboard the incoming helo, the SWAT team leader conversed with Rycroft. She and Rycroft provided eyes for them on their final approach to the landing zone.

Moments later the sound of aircraft engines broke the quiet. The sky was dark overhead, the thick cloud cover blocking the moon. Perfect conditions for an assault.

Through her scope, she spotted the two helos the instant they punched through the cloud deck and dropped into the clearing. The men outside the cabin barely had time to react before the SWAT teams began swarming out of the aircraft.

Dempsey ran into the cabin with three of his guards, while the others scattered like roaches behind cover. A few of the dumbasses fired at the SWAT team.

Briar's pulse remained calm, her breathing slow and steady as she watched the assault, ready to fire the instant she got the command. She kept her eyes on one of the bodyguards who managed to slip around the far right side of the cabin and take shelter behind an old stone shed.

"Target right, two o'clock. Six-hundred-eight yards," Rycroft murmured, his voice as calm as if he was commenting on the weather.

"On him."

The man raised his rifle to his shoulder and took aim at the assault team, clearly thinking he was safe behind cover. But he wasn't. From here she had a perfect view of the side of his head.

She honed in on his ear, adjusted the scope's reticle. Curved her finger around the trigger. And waited.

An ounce or two more pressure...

Just out of her view, one of the SWAT members engaged a bodyguard. The man behind the shed shifted, ready to take a shot. She waited for Rycroft's command.

"Fire," he said.

She squeezed the trigger. The butt kicked into her shoulder, her body absorbing the force of the recoil as the report echoed through the woods. Less than a heartbeat later, her bullet struck the target. His head exploded like a melon and he slumped over, dead before he even hit the ground.

She pulled back the bolt and pushed it forward in one smooth, automatic motion, clearing the chamber and loading the next round.

"Good hit," Rycroft murmured. "Target, eleven o'clock. Six-hundred-two yards."

She shifted the barrel slightly left, found the man he was looking at. "Got him."

But she never got the chance to fire another round.

After a brief exchange of fire between SWAT and the neo-Nazi fucktards, it was over.

"HVT in custody, cabin clear. Sweeping rear area now," the team leader said.

Good deal. Keeping watch just in case, Briar never took her eye from her scope as she scanned the area, looking for more threats they might have missed.

She and Rycroft kept watch until SWAT was done securing the area. Agents loaded the prisoners onto the helos and took off, leaving the scene for the mop-up crews to deal with.

Pushing back into a kneeling position, Rycroft looked over at her, his grin barely visible in the near darkness. "Guess that means the fun's over. Ready to get out of here?"

"Yeah."

They gathered up their gear and hiked back to the dirt bikes they'd hidden before riding out to the closest road where a pickup waited for them. The driver took them to the command center.

After finishing their reports—the part Briar hated but was grudgingly accepting more and more—she and Rycroft each got a hot shower and a mug of coffee, which she declined. Rycroft raised an eyebrow at her in surprise but didn't say anything as she climbed into the SUV. He drove them to the airport where a small private plane awaited them.

She spent the hour-long flight dozing on and off, woke when they came in for their final approach. Yawning, she stretched her arms over her head. Rycroft looked totally alert, as if he'd never slept at all.

He was a handsome, well-built man, even in his fifties. Not that he was anywhere near as gorgeous as Matt. But still. "For an old 'semi-retired' guy, you sure don't need much sleep," she told him.

He grinned, his silver eyes glinting. "It's called parenting. Only the strong survive."

"Yeah? Tougher than, say, Special Forces selection?"

"The sleep deprivation of a new parent makes what I went through to earn my green beret look like a cakewalk. I'm serious."

She huffed out a laugh and followed him off the plane to the small terminal building where an excited squeal startled her. She stopped, watched as a little purple blur streaked around the corner and came at them.

Rycroft dropped his bags, a huge smile lighting his face as he crouched down and held his arms open. "There's my girl," he said, catching Sarah as the raven-haired toddler launched herself into her father's arms.

A bittersweet, poignant pang hit Briar in the center of her chest as she watched them. The deep, incredible bond between them was undeniable, even though they didn't share the same DNA. Love was what made a family, not genetics.

The scene made her think of Matt. He had always wanted to be a father, and she had no doubt he would be amazing at it. Since becoming an orphan at age eight she had longed to be part of a family again.

Matt was her family now and she wanted to have children with him but deep down a tiny part of her worried she wasn't cut out for it. She wasn't exactly maternal. Or normal, for that matter. Kids were fragile and impressionable. She didn't want to be responsible for ruining one.

Grace came around the corner, smiling fondly at her daughter and husband. "She insisted we come to get you," she said to him as she walked up to hug him.

"I'm glad. This is a nice surprise." Still holding Sarah, he leaned down to kiss the crown of his wife's head, the pigtailed toddler snuggled up in his strong arms.

The picture they presented made Briar miss Matt even more.

Sarah made eye contact with Briar over her father's broad shoulder, grinned. "Hi, Briar."

Briar couldn't help but grin back. She wasn't that comfortable around kids or babies, but this one seemed to like her well enough, so maybe there was still hope for her as a parent. "Hey, Sarah."

Rycroft glanced back at her, jerked his head toward the exit. "Come on, we'll give you a lift."

"Thanks, but I've already got a cab coming. You guys go ahead."

He raised an eyebrow. "You sure?"

She nodded. "And maybe get that baby some pancakes on the way home."

Sarah's head popped off her father's shoulder, her black eyes lighting up. "Pancakes? I *love* pancakes."

Rycroft shot Briar a wry look. "Thanks a lot." He shifted Sarah into his left arm and reached down to pick up his bags while Grace wound an arm around his waist. "See you Monday."

"Yeah." Briar waited a moment before following,

giving them some space because being too close to their family unit felt like an intrusion for some reason, then headed for the front doors.

While waiting for her cab, she pulled out her phone to call Matt, but held off. Commander of the FBI's Hostage Rescue Teams, he was still in Colorado handling an op. She didn't want to take the chance of distracting him in any way right now.

Oh, she was *so* looking forward to seeing him when he got home, though she couldn't help but wonder how he would take her news. However it turned out, this reunion was going to be one for the books.

Chapter Two

F eet apart, arms folded across his chest and his lucky
Charger's ball cap on his head, HRT Commander
Matt DeLuca stood in the mobile command vehicle
and kept his gaze glued to the monitor in front of him.
Blue Team was in position on the roof and ready to breach
the veteran's care building to rescue the hostages and
apprehend the suspect on his order.

The camera angle sucked. There was too much going
on, too many people moving around while police cleared
the area for him in the shot to get a good look at the
building. He tapped his earpiece to contact the team.
"Tuck, gimme a sitrep."

"Perimeter's secure," the team leader answered calmly
in his Alabama drawl. "Nothing more from inside."

After killing the first hostage over an hour ago, the
suspect had gone quiet. The team had been en route to the
site at the time.

Matt was aware of all the people around him as he
studied the scene. Mostly FBI and local police. He didn't
spare them so much as a glance, all his focus on his team

and the unfolding situation.

They would have to do a direct assault. A former soldier suffering from PTSD had snapped yesterday, storming the facility where he had previously received treatment, and taken employees hostage. Matt wanted the perp neutralized one way or the other before he took any more innocent lives. "Breach authorized. It's your call."

"Roger. Stand by."

Matt switched his attention to the screen on the right, showing a feed from Tuck's helmet cam. As team leader, Tuck's place was at the back of the column, giving Matt a good view of the other six guys.

"On my mark," Tuck murmured to his teammates. "Three. Two. One. Execute."

Evers rammed the door open with a breaching tool. Bauer's huge silhouette plunged through it, followed by the rest of the team. The seven-man-team swept the staircase leading to the lower floor of the care home.

"Clear," Schroder said.

"Moving to hallway," Tuck said.

Matt stayed silent, letting them do their thing. He felt like he was with them as he watched the infrared feed from Tuck's camera.

His heart rate increased slightly as they rushed down the hall toward the room where the suspect was likely holed up with the remaining hostages, but he didn't budge. Watching from the sidelines was the hardest part of this job. He'd much rather have been part of the assault but his days as a sniper and operator were long behind him now.

The team cleared three rooms before reaching the one the suspect was thought to be in.

The camera bobbed slightly as Tuck nodded at one of his teammates. Bauer reared back and slammed his boot into the door just beside the lock. It flew open, the team streaming into the room before it hit the wall.

"FBI," Tuck shouted over top of shrill female screams. The feed showed three female hostages cowering in one corner of the room behind a large desk, their hands behind their backs.

Tuck's head whipped around. The male suspect stood in the opposite corner, an arm locked around the fourth female hostage's neck, a pistol to her temple. "Drop your weapon!"

More screams pierced the tense silence as the suspect refused to comply. Then he angled the pistol at his own head.

Two shots exploded simultaneously.

The suspect dropped, dragging the female hostage with him. Her sharp, short scream cut off, then turned into muffled sobbing.

Tuck stood his ground while two other team members rushed forward. The sound of a scuffle ensued, quickly ended.

Then quiet.

"Suspect deceased," Tuck announced a moment later. "Room clear. All remaining hostages secured."

Matt allowed himself a deep breath. "Copy that. Anyone hurt?"

"Remaining hostages appear okay. Schroder's looking at them now."

"Copy. Good work." It was always such a relief when ops went this smoothly, though they rarely did, and he was acutely aware of the lives taken today.

It took a couple more hours to get everything wrapped up on his end so he could debrief the team, file the paperwork and head for the airport. He called Briar on the way but got her voicemail. He wasn't even sure if she was home yet. For all he knew, she was still in West Virginia with Rycroft, who understandably couldn't seem to take that final step into retirement. She loved working with him because she got to put her impressive and deadly skill set to use.

"Hey, it's me. All good here and I'm on my way home. You back yet? Should be there by seven or so. Love you."

He slid his phone back into his pocket and leaned his head back to take a snooze. The Bureau-chartered plane was still on the runway but the rest of the guys were already sound asleep in their seats.

All except for Schroder, who was staring out the window at the runway like his life depended on it, hands gripping the armrests in what Matt was sure was a death grip.

And no wonder, given what had happened a few months back.

Matt got up and walked back to take the seat next to Schroder. This was the second flight they'd taken since the crash that had nearly cost Schroder his life and temporarily blinded him, so no surprise he was having a tough time. Matt had been so wrapped up in intel reports on the hostage situation on the way down here that he hadn't thought to check on his medic. "This is like flying first class compared to a C-130, huh?"

Schroder acknowledged him with a forced smile and broke eye contact, clearly embarrassed as he released the armrests and folded his arms. "Yeah."

The plane's engines powered up and they began their acceleration down the runway. Schroder visibly tensed. Matt hadn't been with the team when the C-130 carrying them hit a civilian drone and crashed on takeoff. Matt glanced past him out the window. "Nothing but clear blue sky out there."

"I'm good," Schroder said without looking at him.

The plane's nose lifted and Schroder was still rigid in his seat. Matt needed to distract him. "Won't get much sleep when you get home now that you've got a newborn in the house. You should take advantage while you can."

Schroder glanced at him as the plane lifted into the

sky, then across the aisle at Bauer and Tuck, who were both fast asleep. "I gave Bauer a hard time about the whole fatherhood thing just before the accident that day. But he was right about the no sleep thing. Don't want him to see me crumble."

Matt chuckled. "He's out cold, and you should be too. How's Taya doing with you being away the first time since little man came along?"

A soft smile dissolved the tension on the former PJ's face. "She's in her glory. Tired, but loving it. We both are. I can't wait to get home."

"Glad to hear it."

The plane shuddered as they hit a pocket of turbulence. Schroder's face tightened briefly, his gaze darting back out the window.

Matt stretched his legs out. "Mind if I sit here for the rest of the flight? More leg room in this row."

As he'd intended, Schroder looked back over at him. "Of course, go ahead."

"Thanks."

Schroder looked out the window again but the plane was climbing steadily now, the air smoother. Matt eased his seat back the whopping three inches it allowed and pulled the bill of his cap down over his face, secretly watching Schroder out of the corner of his eye. A minute later the medic finally relaxed, leaned back in his seat and closed his eyes.

Perfect.

After a nonstop two days on the job with little sleep, Matt was tired, but his brain wouldn't stop spinning. Like Schroder, he couldn't wait to get home. He missed his wife.

They'd only been apart five days this time, which was nothing. But something had been nagging at him a while now. He and Briar definitely needed a few days away together to reconnect. They hadn't had much time

15

together as a couple recently, due to their jobs and conflicting schedules.

Not okay. He knew better than most people just how short life could be, and that he couldn't let this pattern continue. He'd lost too much already and made a point of regularly reminding himself what was truly important in life.

His wife. His family, and his teams, who he also considered part of his extended family. Everything else was just distraction and noise.

Briar was still such a mystery to him in a lot of ways, even now after being married for nearly a year. Her past made it hard for her to trust and open up, let alone lean on anyone, including him. It frustrated him sometimes.

He'd also never considered himself to be much of a romantic before, but compared to her he was. So he would take the reins on this one and plan something special for the two of them this week. Although for her, romantic was camping out deep in the woods someplace and shooting together. Was it any wonder why he loved her?

The flight back to Quantico was uneventful. Matt managed to sleep for the last few hours. Schroder even slept through the touchdown.

Matt nudged him awake with his shoulder as they taxied to the end of the runway. "We're here."

Schroder sat up, peered out the window in relief. "Already?"

"Yep. You ready to see Hudson?"

"Can't wait. Bet he's grown since I last saw him."

Matt grinned. His guys were the best and toughest he had ever had the pleasure of commanding, and every one of them went all softhearted when it came to their kids and significant others.

The team unloaded and carried their gear toward the parking lot. Some of the significant others were there waiting. Matt smiled as Bauer, the biggest and hardest of

GUARDED

them all, went all mushy at the sight of his wife and year-old daughter waiting for him there.

Bauer scooped each of them up in a giant arm and started kissing their necks, little Libby's delighted laugh ringing out in the warm spring air. Vance's wife was there as well, along with Cruzie's fiancée.

Matt passed by the others as he headed for his truck, anxious to get on the road. When he stepped out from between two rows of parked vehicles he stopped short.

Briar leaned against the hood of his pickup, her lean body encased in skintight jeans and a formfitting top that made his tongue stick to the roof of his mouth. Her long, dark hair was loose around her shoulders, her deep brown eyes warming as her lips curved upward in a welcoming smile.

"Surprise," she said, straightening and starting toward him with that sexy, confident stride he would never get tired of.

Grinning like an idiot, Matt hurried to her, dropped his bag and dragged her to him for a hug and a deep, thorough kiss.

BRIAR CHUCKLED AGAINST Matt's lips, amused and secretly tickled by the fierceness of his reaction to finding her here. But when he tightened his hold on her and slid a hand up to tangle his fingers in the back of her hair, signaling he was intent on reducing her to a puddle of need right here and now, she went all melty inside. Apparently he'd missed her more than she had realized.

Not only the way he kissed her, that dominant, authoritative hold never failed to rev her libido. He made her feel like the most desirable woman on earth. The hum of anticipation at seeing him burst into flame, setting her body alight. By the time he lifted his head and eased his grip, her entire body pulsed with need.

17

Hands on his broad shoulders, she peered up at him. "That was a pretty great hello, but I came to take you on a dinner date. You up for it?"

His green eyes glowed with latent heat. "I'm up for a lot of things."

She laughed softly and pressed her hips against his, the hard ridge of his erection impossible to miss. Her husband was a damn attractive man. He was also loyal, hardworking and protective. Sometimes she still couldn't believe he'd wanted to marry her. "I can see that. Think you'll live if you have to wait a couple more hours to do something about it?"

"No."

She grinned and drove them to an Asian place she'd been wanting to try that served Korean BBQ. "So things went well in Colorado, I take it?" she asked after the server set their food down.

"Pretty well. Wish we'd been there in time to save the other hostage though."

Briar nodded and managed to wrestle a piece of meat onto her chopsticks. So slippery and frustrating, but she was determined not to cave and use a fork. "Saved the others though."

Matt made a sound of agreement as he swallowed a sip of his beer. "What about you?"

"Got our HVT along with his inner circle and didn't lose anyone. So yeah, good."

He studied her a moment. "Were you directly involved?"

"Recon and overwatch."

He swallowed a mouthful of BBQ chicken, raised a challenging eyebrow. "Nothing else."

One side of her mouth lifted. He knew her too well. "Maybe something else."

"You seem pretty pleased about it," he remarked with a half-grin.

She shrugged. "Might have saved a couple lives." By taking one. Not that she was going to lose any sleep over killing a wannabe Nazi. "You know how it is. All in a day's work." They both had high security clearances but they rarely talked about the specifics of an op until the active investigations surrounding it were closed.

"Uh huh." Matt chuckled and shook his head. "I shouldn't find that so sexy, but I do." Reaching for his beer, he fought back a gargantuan yawn.

"You sleep on the plane?"

"Not much."

"How come?"

"Too busy thinking about you."

She blinked and lowered her chopsticks. "Me? Why?"

A rueful look came over his face, then he chuckled as he shook his head. "Because you're my wife and I missed you."

Awww. "Well that's nice to hear. I...missed you too." She resisted the urge to glance around and make sure no one had overheard her.

Now his eyes laughed at her. "One day you're going to be able to say it without sounding like you're choking."

She flushed. She was trying to be more comfortable with telling him how she felt, she really was. "I didn't sound like I was choking."

He let it go. "You about done there?" He nodded at her plate, an unmistakable gleam of male interest in his eyes.

"Someone's in a hurry. And no, I'm not. I'm starving." She stuffed another bite into her mouth. "I'm thinking a little delayed gratification is good for you."

"That's where you're wrong." He turned and flagged down their server to pay the bill while Briar finished everything on her plate.

She drove them home after. When she glanced over at him a few minutes in, Matt was fast asleep, his head resting on the passenger window. He wasn't a napper, so he must be exhausted. Her heart squeezed at the proof that a man like him trusted her enough to completely relax and let himself go that way.

He woke when she slowed in front of their house and the front tires of the truck bumped over the edge of the driveway, inhaled deeply as he straightened in his seat. Going from deep under to totally alert in the space of a heartbeat, the result of spending his entire adult life in elite military service to his country. She was exactly the same.

Pulling into the garage, tiny jitters fluttered in her belly. A little nervousness, a lot of excitement. Would he react the way she'd imagined?

She followed him up to their bedroom, sat on the bed while he took his bag into their closet. For the past few hours she had thought over and over about how to tell him. Some women came up with cute or clever ways to do it. That wasn't her. So she would just tell him straight up.

He came out of the walk-in, nodded toward the attached bathroom and raised an eyebrow. "I'm gonna grab a shower. You wanna join me?"

She smiled. "Maybe."

He disappeared into the bathroom. The shower ran. She waited until she heard the shower door open, then got up and followed him. The sight that greeted her was more than worth the wait.

Matt stood facing away from her under the spray, the muscular glory of his back, shoulders and ass on perfect display. Mmmm, she would never tire of that view.

As if he sensed her stare, he angled a look over his shoulder at her. "Coming?"

"Not yet," she answered with a coy little smile. "But hopefully soon."

He beckoned her closer with a jerk of his head. "Get that sexy ass in here." The heated, absorbed look he gave her sent heat punching through her.

She left her clothes where they fell on the floor, then stepped into the shower with him. The door hadn't yet shut completely when he spun around to grab her around the hips and hoisted her off the floor. With one quick move he had her pinned to the wet tile wall with his hard, aroused body.

Briar wrapped her legs around his waist, smiling as he buried his face in the side of her neck and growled, both hands palming her butt. Oh yeah, he'd *really* missed her. "I have something to tell you," she said before things inched closer to the point of no return.

"Later," he muttered, dragging his tongue down her neck.

She shivered, closed her eyes a second. *No. Wait.* "I really think you want to hear this now." She tugged at his hair. "Matt."

With a groan he stopped and lifted his head to stare down at her with those hungry green eyes. "Fine, I'm listening. What?"

She bit the edge of her lower lip for a second, hesitating, savoring the anticipation as the moment stretched out. "I'm pregnant."

He froze, seemed to even stop breathing as he stared at her, his expression going blank with astonishment. "What? Are you sure?"

She nodded, praying he would be as excited about this as she'd hoped. Of the two of them, he was the natural parent. She had a steep learning curve to navigate before the baby was born. "I took two tests when I got home. Both positive. I'll go to the doctor to double check and make sure everything's okay, but yeah. Looks like we're having a baby."

An elated smile broke over his face, filling her with warmth. "Oh my God," he said on a laugh. He pressed his face into her hair, curving those hard, powerful arms around her hips to hold her tight. Another soft laugh shook him. "I can't believe it."

Smiling, she stroked his hair. "I know, it happened really fast." Way faster than she had expected. Now it was a bit of a shock to the system, with the ultimate deadline looming in the distance. In less than a year from now, her whole world would change.

Matt eased her feet to the floor and straightened to stare down at her. His eyes were wet, and not from the shower.

Oh... Something caught in her chest. The sight of her strong, commanding husband standing there with tears in his eyes because he was overwhelmed with emotion turned her heart upside down.

"Don't cry," she murmured, wrapping her arms tighter around him.

He shook his head and slid an arm around her back, stroking her wet hair away from her face. "I just... I'm overwhelmed."

Briar rested her cheek on his sturdy shoulder, loving him even more, thrilled that the news had made him so happy. "I know. Me too." It thrilled her to be able to give them this. Matt had wanted a family for a long time and he'd been through so much, losing his first wife while she was pregnant with their child.

He'd grieved for them for a long time, and though he had moved on with Briar, he would never completely get over that loss. She had struggled with that initially, due to her own insecurities that she kept well buried, but now she understood why it would always affect him and didn't begrudge him for it.

She kissed the edge of his jaw, rubbed her cheek against the rough stubble there. "So you're happy?"

He nodded and hid his face against her hair again, seemed to struggle with himself as he held her.

It made her smile. She had known he would be deeply

affected by the news, hoped he would be happy, but he was even more emotional about it than she had expected.

After a long moment he released her and eased back to blow out a deep breath. "How are you feeling?"

"Fine. Little tired, but not sick. I'm actually hungry all the time."

He splayed a big hand over her abdomen, his expression awed. "How far along are you?"

"Almost five weeks."

"So you're due when?"

"Early January, I think. I'll find out for sure when I see the doctor."

A crease formed in the middle of his forehead. "What about your heart?"

There was no mistaking the deep concern behind the question, or the reason for it. "Matt, my heart is fine. I'm *fine*."

He didn't look convinced. "When do you see the doctor?"

"Thursday morning."

He nodded once, his eyes burning with that familiar protectiveness she recognized all too well. "I'm coming with you."

"Hey." She reached down to take his hand. Laced their fingers together. "Babe, I'm fine. Everything's gonna be fine."

"Yeah."

But he didn't sound convinced and she knew him better than anyone walking this earth. And so she sensed the buried fear warring with the protectiveness in him. The ghosts of his former loss fighting with the vow to her written in his gaze. *I won't let anything happen to either of you.* "Are you happy too?" he asked.

"Yes." She lowered her gaze to the center of his sculpted chest, his HOG's tooth bullet resting on his wet skin. "I'm nervous too. I don't know anything about how to be a mother, and barely know anything about kids. I don't want to screw it up."

She had only a handful of memories of her own mother, and fewer still of her father. After losing them in the car accident she had been taken straight into the Valkyrie Program. There had been no nurturing there. Her trainers and handlers had done their best to turn her into a stone cold killer with her rifle, deprogramming any maternal instinct she might have had out of her. For their baby's sake, she hoped there was still a bit of it buried inside her somewhere.

Matt tucked a finger beneath her chin and tipped her face up until she made eye contact. "You're going to be a fantastic mother."

She sure as hell hoped so. But his confidence in her was a definite boost. "Well, I figure if I can love you this much, then maybe I have what it takes after all."

He made a sound of agreement and sank to his knees in front of her to rub his face against her lower belly. Her stomach was still flat as ever. It was so weird to think there was a baby growing inside her.

Matt kissed the spot below her belly button, his lips warm, lingering there. Arousal pulsed through her blood, heady and sweet.

With a saucy smile she threaded a hand through his hair and gave it a tug to make him move lower. "Seeing as I've already got you down there on your knees..."

He looked up at her, amusement and desire glowing in his eyes. "So bossy," he murmured, curving his hands around to cradle her bottom. Holding her with a firm grip so she couldn't move away as he kissed lower, lower.

A thrill shot through her bloodstream, her body tightening in anticipation of his tongue. "You love that about me."

He made a low sound of agreement and then her thoughts scattered as he lowered his mouth between her parted thighs.

Chapter Three

If anyone had asked her two years ago whether she could ever have envisioned herself voluntarily attending a baby shower where she was surrounded by a dozen women cooing over baby outfits, Briar would have either laughed her ass off or assumed that person was nuts. Yet here she was, against all odds. Though there wasn't much she wouldn't do for Taya.

And the strangest part was, she didn't hate it even a tenth as much as she would have back then. These women were her friends now. A kind of extended family she'd never imagined having until Matt had come along and reframed her entire world. If she could just get through the event without anyone questioning her about refraining from caffeine or alcohol, she would consider it a win. She and Matt wanted to keep their news quiet until the first trimester was over. But these ladies were sharp.

"Zoe, quit hogging my baby and hand him over to someone else," Taya chided as she passed by Briar with an empty platter on her way to the kitchen.

Bauer's wife looked up, her heavily made-up golden eyes widening in bewilderment. "What? I've only had him for ten minutes," she protested in her soft Louisiana drawl.

"*This* time," Taya said laughingly. "You're terrible at sharing."

Zoe's expression fell, then softened as she looked down at the baby. "I know, but they're just so sweet and tiny and...*edible* when they're newborns," she said, snuggling Hudson to her floral gothic skull shirt, clearly in no hurry to give him up.

"All right, that's it." Summer got up from the overstuffed chair in the corner, marched over and held her hands out for the baby. "Hand him over. That edible comment makes me concerned for his safety. I don't trust you with him."

Zoe huffed. "As if." Reluctantly she handed Hudson over, her gaze following him through the room as Summer walked away, cooing to him.

"My God, you really do look like you want to eat him up," Rachel said with a laugh, leaning back into the couch with her glass of wine.

"I know." Zoe reached for the plate of food she had abandoned. "I'm totally ready for another one."

"I think Clay might have something different to say about that," Taya teased. "Even if you're ready, according to Nathan, he wasn't a fan of the birthing process. The man's still psychologically traumatized from Libby's birth."

"*He's* traumatized? Okay." Zoe laughed, a low, throaty sound as sultry and exotic as she was. "He's so funny."

Funny? Briar didn't think of Bauer as funny. The man was hard as iron, barely ever cracked a smile, and if he did, it was almost always for his wife and child. "Need a hand in here?" she asked Taya in the kitchen.

"Sure, you can help me get the rest of these appetizers out of the oven."

Briar grabbed for the oven mitts. "How come you're doing all this, anyway? I thought showers meant the new mama sat on a throne while everyone else did her bidding."

"Nah, that's not my style, and I'm actually feeling pretty rested. I pumped two bottles so Nathan could take over the overnight feedings last night, so whatever the guys are doing together right now at Zoe and Clay's place, he's probably asleep on the couch in the middle of it. Plus all of you brought something for the potluck, so it's not like I've been slaving away in the kitchen or anything."

Still. "Let me do this, and go sit down."

Taya shot her a knowing grin, her gray eyes twinkling. "You just want an excuse to hide in here by yourself."

She totally did. Even though socializing with the team and significant others had become easier for her since she'd first been with Matt, it was still outside of her comfort zone. Her formative years had been spent honing her introverted tendencies and using them to make her into a lethal sniper. It wasn't easy to undo all that programming. "I'm getting better, though."

"Yes, you are, and we appreciate that you keep showing up to the get-togethers." Taya playfully nudged her with her shoulder. "All right, if you're sure, I'll leave you to it in here." She plucked her glass of wine off the countertop. "Only one I'm allowing myself, so I'm going to make it last and enjoy every drop. You want one?"

"No, I'm good." Of all the HRT women, Briar was closest to Taya. The woman was the kindest, most nurturing person Briar had ever met. Just being in her presence was soothing, like having a hug or fresh chocolate chip cookies warm from the oven. They had become pretty close over the last year or so. She and Matt had been the only guests outside of Taya's immediate family at her and Schroder's wedding.

In fact, the only woman Briar was closer to was her

fellow ex-Valkyrie, Trinity. Mostly because of their shared history, a lot of it the opposite of pretty. Then there was Georgia, but they didn't hear from her much. The three of them were still inextricably linked, however. Going through something that intense together created a bond for life.

Briar carried the tray of hot appies out to the table where the team's significant others were all gathered around admiring the baby gifts and enjoying the food. "Go easy on the cheese dip, it's the only bowl of it we've got," she said, placing it in the center of the table.

Everyone dug in immediately. Summer looked up at her, baby Hudson expertly cradled in one arm. "Here, you better take your turn holding him now, while Zoe's busy stuffing her face," she teased, and stood to offer Hudson to her.

Briar blocked the immediate impulse to decline and step back. Babies were cute enough. Well, some of them. But they were also terrifyingly tiny and fragile. She'd held Libby and Sam a few times when they were small, though not often, and every single time she'd felt awkward and scared she might drop them. But now that she was about to be a mother herself she had a hard deadline to overcome that anxiety by and lots to learn before her due date, so she might as well get moving on both.

"Okay." She reached for Hudson, wrapped in his little receiving blanket. She frowned in concentration as she carefully handled the transfer from Summer's practiced arms. She slid a hand under his little head, her other forearm beneath his back, and cradled him close. The baby didn't so much as twitch, sound asleep.

Briar studied his sweet little face. Jeez, he was tiny. And warm. He fit right in the crook of her arm. And he was so damn sweet in sleep, the little crescents of his auburn eyelashes forming shadows on the tops of his cheeks...

"Aww, look at you," Carmella said. "You're smitten."

Briar flushed and stood there holding the baby while the women all watched her with fond, teasing smiles. But he was so cuddly. He even smelled good. "I am."

"See? You're a natural," Taya said, giving her a big smile.

It sure felt good, holding him. Satisfying in a way she couldn't describe. Would it be even more intense to hold her own baby in a few months?

Her turn didn't last long. Marisol took Hudson next, leaving Briar to resume serving the food and then begin the cleanup. As the shower wrapped up everyone carried the dishes into the kitchen and took a turn cuddling Hudson before leaving.

Briar stayed behind to help Taya finish tidying up. The moment Taya locked the door behind the last guest she turned toward Briar, Hudson in her arms, and lifted a dark eyebrow, her dark curls spilling over one shoulder. "All right, what's the deal?"

Briar blinked at her. "Huh?"

"Don't 'huh' me. You didn't touch the wine or the coffee, even though you're a known caffeine addict, and you willingly held my child for longer than a minute. You even enjoyed it." She cocked her head, ran an assessing gaze over Briar's middle. "Are you...?"

Shit. For a civilian, Taya was too damn observant. It was on the tip of Briar's tongue to deny it, but she adored and trusted Taya, and she didn't see the point in lying to her. Taya would see straight through it. "Yeah."

Those pretty gray eyes widened in surprise, white showing all around the irises. "You are? Oh my God, congratulations!" She broke into a joyous smile and crossed to her.

Briar couldn't help but grin as Taya gave her a one-armed hug, careful not to squash Hudson between them. "Thanks. But don't tell anyone. I just found out and told

Matt last night. He doesn't want anyone to know until after the first trimester. It's early yet, and after what he went through with Lisa, he wants to wait, because…"

Taya lowered her arm and stepped back, her face somber now. "I understand. How did he take it?"

"He's happy. Really happy." Remembering his reaction put a warm glow in the center of her chest.

"Aww, he's going to be a fantastic daddy."

"He is."

Taya tilted her head to study her. "And what about you? Are you excited?"

She shrugged, not wanting to make a big deal of it. But yeah, she was. "A little. It still feels surreal though."

"Nervous?"

Briar chuckled. "Maybe a tiny bit."

Taya grinned. "I know how hard it was for you to admit that, so thank you for your honesty."

She couldn't help but chuckle. "You know me too well."

"True."

"So you won't tell anyone?"

"Of course not. Except for Nathan. You can't make me keep it a secret from him."

"All right, but you have to make him swear he won't tell anyone."

"I will. I'll make him cross his heart and hope to die, stick a needle in his eye and all that if he tells."

Briar fiddled with the end of the dishtowel in her hands. "Do you think the others are suspicious? Maybe they noticed the coffee thing?"

"No. Don't worry."

Okay, good. She relaxed and resumed doing the dishes while Taya gingerly sank onto a stool at the island to feed the baby.

"Still a little sore down there," her friend said with dry smile, draping a blanket-thingy for nursing over herself and the baby. "But I think we've at least got the hang of this breast-feeding thing now." She flinched, shifted the baby. "Yep, he's definitely got the latch part down."

Briar frowned. She'd never thought about the mechanics of breastfeeding until just now. Would it be weird? "Does it hurt?" She hadn't known it hurt.

"*Yes*. At least it has for me so far. But I'm told that will get better soon." Taya waved a hand in dismissal. "You'll be fine. Don't worry, I'll tell you *all* the things nobody tells you about having a baby before it's your turn."

Briar glanced over at her friend occasionally as she washed up. The pure joy and contentment on Taya's face as she looked down at her baby made Briar happy. If anyone had ever been meant to be a mother, it was Taya. In terms of parents, Hudson couldn't have done any better. "You make it all look so natural."

Taya grinned. "Do I?" She shifted Hudson on her shoulder, patting his back to burp him, and the baby emitted the most adorable squeak from under the blanket. "Well then, I'm glad. I've wanted this for as long as I can remember. But the truth is, as far as parenting goes, we all figure it out as we go, I think. Women have been having babies since the dawn of mankind, after all. We just know what to do because it's instinct."

Did she have those instincts, after everything she'd gone through? Briar wasn't sure.

She watched her friend, wanting to talk more but unsure if she should or not. Confiding in anyone was hard for her. Even confiding in her husband. It took a conscious effort on her part to open up about her feelings, and she didn't do it often.

Taya was so easy to talk to, though. And she was so freaking *nice*. So Briar pushed aside the nagging sense of guilt and vulnerability and opened up about the insecurities that were nagging her. "I hope I figure it all out when it's my turn."

"You will. Biology takes over. It's amazing."

"I hope so."

Taya looked up from Hudson with a frown. "Wait, are you really worried about it?"

Briar lowered her gaze. Admitting something like this was hard because insecurity and self-doubt were forms of weakness. She despised weakness, had been trained never to show it. Ever. And if she had, she'd been punished in ways that made her never want to do it again.

"My training...changed me. Inside and out. They took all the softness out of me." She barely remembered her own parents, or the love they must have given her. She didn't want to find out there was none left when the baby came.

Taya made a distressed sound, her expression turning to outrage. "Of course there's still softness in you. I wish you could have seen your face when you held Hudson earlier. Even Carm saw it. And then there's the way you look at Matt. The way you treat him, and the rest of us. There's a lot of softness inside you. I also can't imagine any mother being more fiercely protective of their baby than you will be." She shook her head slowly. "You have such a capacity for love, Briar. You just need to trust yourself more."

I don't know if I can. The niggling thought sent a cold shock of dread through her. She forced a smile anyway. "Working on it. It's all good, I've got lots of time before my little one makes an appearance."

Hopefully by the time the baby came, she would have figured it all out. She was smart, and strong. She could handle it.

After hugging Taya goodbye and giving Hudson a kiss on the top of his dark-haired little head that smelled of baby shampoo, Briar headed home. A few minutes later, her cell rang with Trinity's distinctive ringtone. Returning Briar's call from earlier.

"Hey, you home right now?" Briar asked her.

"Just got in. Where are you?"

"On my way home from Taya's." She hesitated a moment. "Can I drop by for a bit?"

"Sure. Everything okay?"

"Yeah, everything's good. I'll be over in ten."

Trinity opened the front door wearing a pair of skinny jeans and a ruby red tunic that hugged every gorgeous curve, her shiny black hair curling loose around her shoulders. "Long time no see," she said, wrapping Briar up in a hug.

"Yeah, it has been. You just get home from a trip?" Trinity did contract work for the NSA now, courtesy of Rycroft recruiting her. Nothing as invasive or dangerous as what she had done before, though.

"Work thing," Trinity said, leading her into the living room where she sank into an oversize chair and curled her legs up beneath her. "So? To what do I owe the pleasure?"

Briar sat on the couch across from her, unsure how to begin. "Well... I'm pregnant."

Trinity's face froze, then her eyes widened in shock. "You are?"

It was kinda funny how surprised everyone had been so far. "Just found out. It's still early, so don't say anything to anyone. I wanted to tell you in person though."

A tiny frown creased Trinity's brow. "I didn't know you guys were trying."

She also hadn't told Trinity she and Matt wanted to start a family. "We haven't been for long. It kind of just happened."

Her friend gave her a warm smile and got up from the chair. "I'm so happy for you." She engulfed Briar in a big hug, the soft scent of her perfume swirling around them. "Such great news."

"Thank you," she murmured, flushing. She hated

being the center of attention, it made her feel awkward. "Anyway, now you know."

"I'm glad you told me. And I'm guessing Matt is beyond thrilled?" Trinity sat back down.

"I think so." She knew so.

Trinity was still smiling at her, but there was something in her eyes that bothered Briar. A hint of sadness. Or maybe a deeply buried longing.

And then it hit her.

Oh God, she was so stupid. Briar sucked in a breath, feeling like an asshole. "Ah, shit, Trin. I'm sorry."

Trinity blinked. "What? Why?"

"I didn't think. I wanted to come tell you, and I didn't stop to think that it would be hard on you—"

"Briar. It's fine. I really am happy for you." She put on another smile, and this time whatever Briar had seen in her eyes was gone.

Maybe Trinity was happy for them. But she knew her friend was putting on a brave face for her right now. The Valkyrie Program had cost them all so much. For Trinity, that included the chance to ever have a baby of her own. A forced hysterectomy before she had graduated from the training program had served as an efficient and ruthless way to ensure that biology never posed an inconvenient side-effect while she performed her intimate and up-close assignments.

Of the three of them, without a doubt Trinity had suffered the most. It was a stark reminder that Briar needed to put aside any stupid uncertainties about becoming a mother, and focus on just how lucky she was to have the opportunity.

****

Matt crossed his arms over his chest and fought the urge to pace as he waited for the doctor with Briar in the exam room. Not Briar's regular doctor. The obstetrician Taya had seen during her pregnancy. Matt wanted his wife to have the best care possible.

Briar was lying on the table in a paper gown, hands folded atop her middle as she stared up at the ceiling. She seemed calm and happy about the pregnancy. While he was trying not to let his worry show.

The longer they waited in here, the more time he had to think about all the things that could go wrong. He'd been here once before, only to have his world come crashing down on top of him. If he lost Briar and the baby this time, he wouldn't survive it.

When the ball of anxiety in his gut had turned to a lump of dread, the doctor finally arrived. A young woman in her early thirties.

"Sorry I'm late. Had to check on one of my first time mamas who just went into labor at the end of my rounds." She smiled at them, glanced at her chart. "Got the results of your blood work," she said cheerfully. "Everything looks good. And yes, you're definitely pregnant. Now let's get your vitals checked and do a quick exam."

Matt lowered himself into the chair in the corner and watched while the doc checked Briar over, forcing his concern to the background.

"Blood pressure is perfect," the doc said, removing the earbuds for her stethoscope and unwrapping the cuff from Briar's upper arm. "How are you feeling? Breasts tender?"

Briar blushed and kept staring at the ceiling. "A little."

"That's normal. Any nausea?"

"No. I'm actually hungry all the time."

"Well that's a nice change of pace for me," the doc teased, palpating Briar's abdomen. "Fatigue is normal for the first trimester as well."

"When's the due date?" Matt asked.

"Your wife wasn't exactly sure about the date of her

last period, but based on the blood work and other symptoms, I think right around Christmas."

A Christmas baby. Wow. How amazing was that? "And what about her heart?" he asked, nodding at Briar.

The doctor stopped and looked at him in surprise. "What about it?"

Matt frowned. Had Briar not told her? "She's got an arrhythmia."

The doctor flipped through the pages of Briar's chart. "I didn't hear anything suspicious just now." She scanned the notes, her eyes widening. "Wow, a Taser?" She looked at Briar. "That must have been pretty scary."

Briar shrugged as though the incident had been no big deal, when her heart had fucking stopped beating and Matt had died inside, watching helplessly as Schroder tried to revive her. He'd aged fifty damn years in those few minutes. "I don't really remember most of it. And anyway, it was a freak, isolated incident. I'm fine. And I don't plan on getting Tased again anytime soon." She shot him a warning look.

Matt stared back at her. She was fine when the doc said she was fine, and not until.

"I don't see any cause for concern," the doc said, and Matt relaxed a little. "We'll keep our eye on everything as the pregnancy progresses. It's likely too early to hear baby's heartbeat just yet, but for now I'd say everything looks perfect."

It had with Lisa, too.

No one had known about the aneurysm that would claim her and their baby's life a few short weeks later, right when they had been ready to announce their happy news to everyone. But Briar had a known preexisting condition. What if the strain of the pregnancy made the arrhythmia worse? It could cause a blood clot, and in turn a heart attack or stroke.

The thought of it made him go cold all over. He

couldn't go through that again. He wouldn't survive it.

Oblivious to his thoughts, the doctor smiled at them both before turning back to Briar. "Have you got your prenatal vitamins?"

"Yes." She sat up, tugged the flimsy exam gown around her more securely.

"Good. Well, unless either of you have questions, I'll say congratulations and let you go."

Matt had a thousand more questions, but that warning look from Briar made him keep his mouth shut. For now. All good news so far. They should be celebrating.

He held the clinic door for her as they left, noted the relieved breath she let out when they stepped outside into the fresh spring air. "So, Christmas, huh?" he said.

An almost dreamy smile crossed her face. "Looks like. Guess this means I don't have to get you a gift, right?"

"Yeah, I think giving me a child is pretty much the gift to end all gifts, so anything else on top of that would be a waste of effort and money."

She was quiet until he steered out of the parking lot. "So you heard what she said. Everything looks normal. I'm fine."

He nodded. "I know." But until the baby was born safely, he wasn't going to be able to breathe easy. He would just have to keep all that to himself until the pregnancy was over. "What about Rycroft? Have you told him?"

"Not yet, I wanted to see the doctor first. I'll call him later today."

"You decided what you're gonna do about work yet?"

She gave him a startled look. "What do you mean?"

He would have thought it was obvious. "Well, you can't do fieldwork anymore. Have you thought about what else you want to do instead?"

She arched a dark eyebrow, chin up. "I can't? Says who?"

Her reaction took him off guard. Was she serious? He was already on edge, and her stubborn defiance pissed him off. She and their baby were too important to him. There was no goddamn way he would let her do fieldwork from here on.

"Me," he said tightly. From day one he had learned to pick his battles with her, but fuck. Briar didn't know how *not* to push herself. She needed to put the baby's welfare before her career. And if he had to go over her head and make Rycroft take her out of the field, then so be it.

A tense, loaded silence ensued while Briar kept staring at him. Finally she spoke. "I get that you're worried about me and the baby. But I'm not reckless, and I'm not going to do something that would jeopardize our child's safety. That said, I think I can decide for myself when it's time to retire from the field. You don't get to dictate what I can and can't do." The last words were hard, a cold, flinty edge to her tone.

With effort Matt bit back the retort that leapt to the end of his tongue. Clenching his jaw, he battled back the sudden spike in his temper.

Briar was the last woman on earth who would allow herself to be coddled or protected, let alone dictated to. Where she was concerned he definitely had to dial back the protective, alpha male instinct that was such an ingrained part of him. He knew this about her. She was used to pushing herself, sometimes way past the limit. But goddamn it, it made him nuts that he couldn't make her be more cautious right now.

"Hello?" she prompted when he didn't answer.

"I think we should change the subject," he said, his tone hard.

Before one of them said something that would escalate this into a full out battle. Because as far as he could see, neither of them were going to change their stance on the issue. So the less said on the subject for now, the better.

Chapter Four

Six months later

"You're really doing this?"

At the shock and outrage in Matt's tone, Briar's spine stiffened as she reached for another sweater on the shelf that would fit over her growing belly. "Yup." The red one was stretchy, and wouldn't take up too much room in her suitcase.

His silent disapproval beat against her back as she continued gathering items to pack. When she turned around to exit their walk-in closet, he was blocking her way, a scowl on his face, hands on his hips.

She really would rather not have this fight again. "Excuse me."

He stared at her for a long, tension-laced moment before reluctantly easing aside enough to let her pass, only to follow her over to the bed where she began putting the new items into her open suitcase. "You know you shouldn't be flying this late in the pregnancy."

It took all her restraint to keep from spinning around

and giving him a piece of her mind. "We've been through this. I'm healthy, and I already got permission from the doctor." Besides some normal physical discomfort here and there at this stage of the pregnancy, everything was progressing normally except for the low-lying placenta her OBGYN was keeping an eye on.

He cursed under his breath. "I don't believe this."

Believe it, buddy. It's happening. She was proud of herself for not saying it aloud. When they'd first gotten together, she would have flung the words right in his handsome face.

"You just gonna ignore me?"

"Until you lose the attitude, yep." Okay, maybe she wasn't as evolved as she'd thought, because she got a tiny bit of pleasure out of delivering the jab.

"My attitude that has everything to do with wanting to protect you and our baby?"

Oh, he was seriously pissed. She had to stay calm or this would escalate fast. She hated fighting with him. It would put her in a bad mood and make her miserable after she left. "Our baby and I are doing just fine. The doctor said so and signed the papers for the insurance company. I gave them to Rycroft yesterday." Maybe she'd had to coerce the doctor a little, but in the end the woman had still signed them.

"And you didn't stop to think that maybe I should have a say in this? That your opinion isn't the only one that counts around here?"

She bit back the angry words crawling up her throat, but not the irritated sigh. "We've been over this a few times already, and it's getting old. Just because I'm pregnant doesn't mean I'm helpless or that you get to control me." She shot him a warning look over her shoulder before turning back to her task. They were supposed to go away together for a few days once she got back. She hoped he was over his mad by then.

"God dammit," he snapped, and spun around to pace. He rarely did that, and only when he was really worked up inside.

"Look. I already agreed to drop fieldwork and take a desk job a couple months ago. I've made concessions, given up the job I'm best at and enjoy the most, all to protect the baby. If the doctor had said no to this trip, I wouldn't be going." Sure there was an increased risk because of how far along she was, but there was a hell of a big difference between taking sniper assignments and getting on a freaking airplane for a couple hours.

"No, you would have just kept looking until you found a doctor who *would* sign off on it," he accused.

He wasn't wrong. "Matt, just drop this, okay? It's fine. It's a short flight, and I'll only be gone a couple days. The most strenuous thing I'll be doing on this job is dragging my suitcase behind me, and I already promised this is the last time I'll travel until after the baby's born."

He made a growling sound and stopped to face her. The anger in his gaze sliced her inside, but she refused to let him know it. "Don't go." A warning, not a plea. If she did this, she did it against his wishes and without his support.

Too late. "I have to go, my cab's outside and the team's on the way to the airport." She closed her suitcase, zipped it up and started to slide it off the bed but his hand closed over hers on the handle.

His jaw was set, his gaze intense. Full of anger, yes, but she could also see the worry and hurt buried there too. Then resignation. "I'll take it down for you," he muttered.

"Thank you," she said, stepping out of the way.

He wheeled the suitcase out the door, down their front walkway to the street, where the cab was waiting. The driver put it in the trunk and Matt turned to face her as she reached the curb. His expression was closed now, and her heart hurt. She didn't want him to shut her out, she wanted him to support her.

"Have a safe trip," he said in a clipped tone, and dropped a cool kiss on her cheek before walking away.

Briar stood there a moment, took a deep breath to gather herself before getting into the cab. She'd won this round, but the small victory felt damned hollow and lonely.

Two days later, she didn't feel any better about the whole thing.

She shifted in her seat in a futile effort to find a comfortable position given the current size of her belly. At almost thirty-four weeks along, it already felt like the baby had shoved all her internal organs aside for its own comfort. Her stomach was now somewhere north of her ribcage, and her bladder was about the size of a kumquat.

And she still had about another two months to go.

Annoyed at herself for complaining about it, even in her head, she turned back to the report she was just finishing up for Rycroft. Everything to do with the pregnancy was all systems go. She should be focusing on that, but instead she was missing her husband.

He was still mad at her. Not icy anymore, he'd been civil enough during their phone conversations and their getaway was still on, but he had been a little cool.

She didn't like it, or the residual tension between them. When Matt had gone with her to their first ultrasound appointment a couple months back, he'd been so excited and she'd never felt closer to him. She even carried their baby's first picture in her wallet. They still didn't know the gender. They both wanted it to be a surprise. Briar was convinced it was a boy.

"About done with that?" Rycroft asked her as he walked into the hotel conference room they were using. The recon op had finished an hour ago, and she and others were working on compiling the reports. Not even remotely her idea of a good time.

"Almost. Just one last section to wrap up." The baby shifted, almost in a somersault beneath Briar's ribs. She glanced down in time to see something poke out beneath the left side of her ribs and trace around to the right, the fabric of her top moving with it. "Someone just woke up. Funny how he sleeps during the day and does gymnastics in there while I'm trying to sleep."

"He?" Rycroft grinned. "I thought you guys weren't going to find out the sex."

"It's definitely a boy. Mother's intuition. And he's already got strong legs."

"Active, just like his mama."

She made a face. "I'm not active anymore. Look at me. I'm like a beached whale sitting here."

"You're not that big yet, Briar. Trust me."

"Well I feel huge." She put a hand to her belly and something bumped into her palm.

A knee maybe. Or an elbow. The first time she'd seen her belly move like that it had freaked her out, but now she found it cool. She liked feeling the baby move inside her. Matt loved to touch her belly all the time too. He would rub it and kiss it, put his head in her lap and talk to the baby. It was ridiculous and adorable at the same time, and made her fall even more in love with him each day. God, she hated that she'd left while they were fighting. Hopefully they could smooth everything over again during their quick holiday.

"We'll head to the airport around three, okay?"

"Sounds good."

He eyed her awkward position in the chair. "I don't know about you, but I'm looking forward to you putting your feet up for a while."

Briar chuckled. "You sound like Matt. I'll put them up for a while, promise." Resting wasn't something she was used to or comfortable with, but she figured she'd earned some.

Things on the home front had improved a lot since she had officially retired from fieldwork. About a month after her belly had popped over the top of her jeans she had finally made the call, much to Matt's relief. She had agreed to work closer to home and keep travel to an absolute minimum now that she was in her last trimester. Being an analyst sucked, though.

"You still going away this weekend?" Rycroft asked her, flipping through a file.

"Yes. Down to North Carolina for four days. Matt booked the time off months ago." He had reserved a room for them at an exclusive B&B on the coast for a getaway. Only a few hours' drive from home, which her increasingly miniscule bladder appreciated.

"Good for you. Glad you're taking some time now. It's busy when the baby first gets here. Everything's different after that."

"I'll bet." She was glad too, even if she did feel a little guilty about it. Once the baby came, her entire world would change.

Normally the thought of sitting around doing nothing for four days would make her nuts but she was looking forward to some downtime and to reconnect with her husband. Even with the improvements in their relationship, it felt like they had been drifting apart a little lately in the ebb and flow of married life, and their demanding work schedules conflicted a lot. The recent fight hadn't helped any. This little holiday was just what they needed.

They loved each other and were willing to put in the ongoing effort a committed relationship required. That didn't come naturally to her but she was trying her best to be a good wife, even if she didn't always agree with him or do what he thought she should. Thankfully Matt hadn't held her shortcomings against her—yet. She was already inexperienced in the whole childcare thing, and she wanted this baby to come home to as solid a home as they could provide.

The flight back to Virginia was uneventful. Rycroft drove her home from the airport. Matt wasn't home from work yet when she arrived. By the time she dragged her suitcase up the stairs she was exhausted. Sleep, or at least solid stretches of uninterrupted sleep, was becoming less and less frequent.

She stripped off everything but her panties and bra and crawled into their king-sized bed for a nap, waking when the mattress shifted sometime later.

Rolling to her other side, she fought her way through the fog of sleep and smiled up at Matt. "Hey," she murmured, trying to get comfortable.

"Hi." He leaned over to kiss her softly, the subtle scent of his crisp cologne teasing her, his comforting welcome filling her with relief. He didn't seem angry anymore. "When did you get home?"

"Five-thirty. What time is it?"

"Just after seven."

Crap. She'd never sleep through the night now. "I only meant to sleep for half an hour."

He eased onto his side next to her and propped his head in his hand, reaching the other out to smooth her hair back. "Ready for a vacay?"

They were supposed to leave first thing in the morning. "Hmmm, yes. You?"

"I can't wait. Been wanting to do this for a long time."

He had? He was so sweet. She really needed to make more of an effort in the whole romance department, do unexpected things that make him feel appreciated more often. She'd gotten a little lazy in that department. "I'm looking forward to spending quality alone time with you." She leaned into him as his mouth came down on hers.

The kiss was slow and dreamy at first, building into something deeper and hotter. His hands stroked over her mostly naked body, lingering to caress the sensitive backs of her thighs as his mouth moved down her jaw to her neck.

She sighed and tipped her head back, her skin tingling all over. Touching him always made her heart beat faster. She slid her hands over his arms, savoring the way his muscles bunched as he shifted closer, then snuck them under the hem of his shirt to slide them over his abs and powerfully defined pecs.

Matt nibbled at the side of her neck, stroked his tongue over a spot that made her shiver, his hand grasping her hip to position her while the other curved around the swell of her breast. She was bigger now by more than a cup size, and more sensitive too. The feel of his fingertips lightly brushing over her nipple through the thin satin bra made her breath catch, sensation zinging through her.

He made an approving sound and kissed his way down her cleavage, rubbing his face against her aching breasts. He tugged the top of one cup down, exposing her.

She closed her eyes, a moan rolling out of her throat when his mouth closed over the rigid peak. He knew exactly what to do, where and how to touch her to make her crazy. She was a little shy about her body now that her belly was so big but he seemed to love it and the way he held her, the way he moved his hands over her made her feel worshipped.

Holding the back of his head to her, she reached her free hand down to cup the bulge at the front of his pants. He pushed into her, rocking back and forth in a rhythm that made her even wetter.

Releasing her breast, he sat up to drag off his shirt, giving her a fantastic view of all the dips and hollows of his muscled torso, then twisted as he shucked off his pants and underwear. She immediately reached for his erection but he caught her wrist and brought her hand to his mouth to nip at the heel.

"Roll over onto your other side," he said in a low, sexy voice that sent a thrill through her.

She turned, arched into his body as he splayed a hand over her belly, the other sliding underneath to play with her breast. His fingertips brushed along the seam of her thighs. Back and forth, light as a sigh, igniting every nerve ending, increasing the throb in her clit. She moved her legs restlessly. He grasped her hip to still her, tugged her panties off, then reached up to grab a pillow and positioned it between her knees.

"Lift up a little," he murmured, pushing her top leg forward, bending her knee to expose her. His mouth was busy at the spot where her neck and shoulder joined, kissing, sucking.

He still didn't give her what she wanted. Instead he continued to tease her with feather-light strokes of his fingers over her thighs, coming close to where she needed them before skipping past over the curve of her belly and back down.

"You plan on teasing me all night?" she finally said, an impatient edge to her tone. He'd gotten her all hot and bothered and seemed in no hurry to put the fire out. Two could play at that game.

But when she tried to turn over, a solid grip on her hip prevented her from moving.

"Stay still," he commanded, the quiet steel in his voice making her breath catch and her toes curl. She loved this game, reveled in how he tested her willpower. She loved it when he took control from her in bed because he was a generous and attentive lover.

He knew exactly how much she loved it, too.

She sank her teeth into her lower lip to bite back a moan as his fingers finally slipped between her thighs from behind and slid along her wet, swollen folds. The moan burst free anyway, a shiver of delight coursing through her.

His other hand was busy playing with her nipple, his mouth hot against her neck. "No. Don't move."

It was nearly impossible to stay still, it felt too good. Her muscles strained with the need to arch into him, to rub his fingers over the spot that ached so badly. He took his time tormenting her, teasing, barely dipping inside her before easing out to stroke her clit.

Over and over until she was gasping, muscles twitching. The orgasm was close now, hovering just out of reach. Tormenting her with its sweet promise of ecstasy.

"Matt," she groaned, managing to stay still only through sheer force of will.

"No."

Dammit, it felt so good but she needed more, and the hard ridge of his erection pressed against her ass was making her even more impatient.

He brought her to the edge two more times, and finally she couldn't take any more.

A plaintive whimper escaped and she reached back to grab his stroking hand, tried to lock her thighs around it to keep him there.

"Such a greedy girl," he whispered against her ear. "You ready to come now?"

"Yes," she blurted, and released his hand to grab his hip, try to drag him closer. She wanted him inside her.

"You want my cock, don't you?"

"*Yes.*"

A low chuckle rumbled through him. "I'll give it to you when I'm good and ready."

Oh Jesus, he was trying to kill her.

She opened her mouth to demand he get on with it already but the words dissolved into a garbled moan as he reached around to the front and found just the right spot on her clit, rubbing until the first stirrings of release tingled at the base of her spine.

Desperate to come, ready to beg, she cried out when he shifted forward and finally pushed inside her. The slow, intimate stretch felt incredible combined with the way he stroked her clit. "Don't ever stop," she commanded him, unsure whether she was threatening or pleading at this point.

"That's my greedy baby," he whispered, his hips moving slow and steady, fingers gliding over her sweetest spot. "Mmm, love the way you clench around me."

The praise, the perfect caresses, the feel of him inside and behind her, triggered her release. She moaned and writhed in his grip, mindless as the pleasure punched through her, prolonged by his lazy strokes. She was gasping for breath when he finally locked his hand around her hip and drove deeper, harder.

He pressed his face into her neck, his harsh breathing hot against her skin. His muffled groan of release sent another shiver through her.

After a few minutes he eased out of her and kissed her shoulder gently. "Stay here," he whispered.

Since she was too tired to move at the moment, she didn't argue. He got out of bed and came back with a damp washcloth for her to clean up with. "Hungry now?" he asked.

She answered with a negative grunt, too content to move. Matt curled around her back and pulled the covers over them both, a solid, hard presence to bolster her. It was dark and quiet, her body warm and relaxed. Within moments she was asleep.

Waking a while later, she sighed and pulled free of Matt's embrace. Nature was calling. She did that a lot now. Sometimes a few times a night.

Swinging her legs over the side of the bed, Briar stood. Warmth gushed between her legs.

She gasped, horrified. *Dammit...*

"What?" Matt asked.

"I think my damn bladder just gave out," she grumbled, and hit the lights to make sure she didn't step in it on the way to the bathroom. God, this was so embarrassing—

A puddle of brilliant red gleamed on the floor.

She paled, a spike of terror shooting through her. "Matt," she said, her voice tight.

He shifted behind her. "What's wrong?"

"I'm bleeding." *Oh, shit. Oh, shit, shit, shit.* There was a lot of it.

"What?" he said sharply, then inhaled when he looked over the side of the bed.

Briar gingerly waddled for the bathroom, heart thudding. "Call my obstetrician. Tell her I'm on the way to the hospital."

Matt was already out of bed and met her before she reached the foot of it. Before she could even open her mouth he had scooped her up in his arms. "Does it hurt?" he asked as he strode for the door.

"No. I didn't feel anything." She put a hand to her belly and stayed still as he carried her. "Wait, I need clothes."

He cursed and quickly reversed directions, heading for the closet.

She grabbed a new pair of panties and a stretchy dress, fighting the fear beating at her. The baby. Was she losing the baby?

Matt shifted her. "Are you still bleeding?"

"I think so." She was afraid to look, but she could feel the wetness. When she did look, there was more between her legs and a thin trail of it on the hardwood floor marking their progress around the room. She swallowed. "I need a pad."

He carried her into the bathroom, set her carefully down on the toilet. More blood rushed into the bowl. Bright red. Fear clutched at her throat. *Oh my God.*

"I'm calling 911," Matt said, phone already in hand as

he dialed.

"No," she said sharply, making him stop and look at her. "It'll take forever for the ambulance to get here. You can get me to the hospital way faster. Just call my doctor and tell her what's going on, so someone there is ready for me."

For a moment it looked like he would argue, but he did as she said, talking to the doctor while she did her best to clean up and put a pad in her new panties. She was in the process of pulling the dress over her head when Matt reached his arms around her again.

"She said to go straight to maternity," he said, lifting her carefully. "They're waiting for you and she's on her way up."

"Okay." Shit, her heart was fucking pounding.

Stop, she ordered herself. The faster her heart beat, the more blood she would lose. She had to calm herself somehow.

Putting a hand to her distended belly, she sent silent messages to the baby. *You're going to be fine. Just hang on. Stay in there.*

Matt rushed down the stairs with her, paused only to shove his feet into his shoes and grab his keys by the door, then carried her into the garage. As soon as he put her in the front seat Briar immediately leaned it back, raising her feet onto the dashboard in an effort to elevate her hips and hopefully slow the bleeding. There were no pains or contractions. What was happening?

Matt hopped in behind the wheel and fired up the engine. "It's gonna be okay," he told her as he reversed fast out of the garage.

Briar didn't answer, too lost in her thoughts, afraid to move… And far more afraid that their baby had already died.

****

Matt drove as fast as he could without putting them at serious risk of getting into an accident as he raced them to the hospital. Part of him thought it was a mistake not to call an ambulance, but Briar was right. They couldn't wait. He could have her to the hospital in a matter of minutes.

He glanced over at her. She was silent, rigid in her seat, her face pale, one hand pressed to her belly. Streaks of drying blood marked the insides of her thighs and calves. What the fuck had happened? Was it the sex? Had he done this?

A car pulled out in front of him. Matt automatically flung an arm out across Briar's chest to keep her from jerking forward as he hit the brakes, then laid on the horn.

Cursing under his breath, ignoring the flung up middle finger from the elderly driver in front of him, Matt kept on the horn until the jackass pulled over. The truck's tires squealed as he hit the gas and raced past the car.

A dark wave of fear rose inside him, threatening to swallow him whole. He pictured Lisa poised on the end of their diving board, sharing a secret smile with him before she jumped into the pool with their nieces.

She had floated to the surface facedown moments later. Already gone, though Matt hadn't known it. Even though he had done everything humanly possible to save her and their baby. Now Briar was bleeding heavily…

He shoved the thought aside, forced back the icy wave of dread flooding his veins. He would not lose Briar or the baby. He couldn't. And he couldn't let her see how fucking scared he was. She needed him to be her rock. He had to hold his shit together, no matter what happened.

She stared unblinkingly through the windshield, her expression anxious. He needed to reassure her.

Reaching over, he pried her left hand free of her belly and squeezed tight. Her skin was cold and clammy.

"Halfway there. Not long now."

She gave a distracted half-nod. "Don't talk. Just hurry."

He was going as fast as he dared already. But with the lives of his wife and child on the line, it didn't feel nearly fucking fast enough.

Chapter Five

Briar had tried every trick she knew to calm down, and nothing was working. She could handle pain. Stress. Hunger. Cold. Sleep deprivation. She had been trained to combat all that a long time ago.

But she wasn't the only one at risk here. She was terrified she had lost the baby. That would devastate her, and maybe Matt even more after all he'd already lost.

She lay on her back on the hospital bed in one of the maternity treatment rooms, a fresh pad wedged between her legs as a nurse came in with a Doppler ultrasound. Matt was waiting out in the hallway. The staff wouldn't let him in right now and Briar didn't want to cause any delays by arguing about it. She could get through this by herself.

Her anxiety spiked when the nurse readied the machine. They already had her hooked up to an IV and were getting ready for a transfusion if necessary. "Let's take a listen," the woman said, squeezing some cold gel onto Briar's abdomen.

Briar held her breath as the nurse placed the probe on her belly and began moving it around.

A strong whooshing noise came through the speaker.

Briar released the breath she'd been holding and all but collapsed back onto the table. The baby's heartbeat sounded strong and regular. Thank God.

"That's good to hear," the nurse said with a smile, then cleaned Briar up and picked up a syringe from the instrument tray. "This is a steroid shot," she said, urging Briar onto her side to pull up the gown and insert the needle into her hip. "Will help with the baby's lung development just in case it's born early."

Holy hell, she couldn't imagine the baby being born this early. "I'm not even thirty-four weeks yet. Would the baby make it?"

The nurse smiled at her. "Let's not get ahead of ourselves. For now everything seems to be settling down. I'm sure it will be fine." She tugged Briar's gown back down and helped her onto her back again. "We'll be taking you down for an ultrasound soon. Hopefully in a few minutes."

The non-answers didn't ease the anxiety. "Can you go tell my husband that the baby's heartbeat sounds good?" She hated to think of him sitting out there wondering whether the baby was still alive or not.

"Of course." She squeezed Briar's shoulder. "Hang in there, mama."

Her doctor finally arrived as the nurse swept out. "Briar. How are you? The baby's heartbeat is strong?"

"Yes. I'm not miscarrying, right?"

"Not, it's likely a placenta previa bleed."

It seemed so unreal. "This happened because my placenta is too low?"

"Right. When you stood up, the pressure caused it to tear, which results in the bleeding." She turned, examined the pad between Briar's legs and the contents of the bedpan one of the nurses had set next to the bed. "You're clotting already, which is a good sign. They're fairly large, though. We'll keep a close eye on you and baby. They're taking you down for an ultrasound soon?"

"Yes."

"We'll know more after that. But for now, baby is hanging tough. As of now you're on strict bed rest until further notice. Limited movement, no sitting up, and you'll have to keep using a bedpan until you're no longer bleeding."

"All right." It was gross and humiliating, but what did any of that matter when her baby's life might still be in jeopardy. She fidgeted with the edge of the blanket at her hip, unable to shake one particular thought that kept circling through her brain. "Is it because I flew yesterday? You told me before this trip that it was a risk because of the position of my placenta."

The doctor had reluctantly cleared her to take the trip, and only after Briar had promised to stay off her feet most of the time. "It was my last flight until after the baby is born. Do you think it caused the bleeding?" The guilt was killing her. Had Matt been right?

The doctor gave her a sympathetic smile. "It's impossible to say, so my advice is not to blame yourself for it."

So it might have. *Oh, Jesus...* Briar exhaled and dragged a hand down her face, suddenly feeling sick to her stomach. What if this was all her fault?

"Briar, it doesn't matter what caused it, and it may have happened whether you had flown or not. Right now we need to focus on stopping this bleeding completely."

Briar glanced down at the hospital gown where spots of blood stained the material at the apex of her thighs. *God.* Matt had been right. He had been so upset with her, had tried to stop her from taking this last trip. She'd gone because it was part of her job, but also, she'd gone because a tiny part of her had bristled at him telling her what to do.

Another shot of guilt made her throat tighten. What the fuck was wrong with her? He only had her and the baby's best interests at heart. Why did she feel the need to fight him on it? She'd been selfish, and now their baby might pay the price for it.

Another nurse came to take her down for the ultrasound. The technician was quiet and thorough during the procedure, and wouldn't tell Briar a thing. "The radiologist will have a look at the results," she told Briar afterward, "then your doctor. She'll discuss them with you."

God, she hated waiting to find out what was happening at a time like this. The baby was alive, but was it all right? Or had something else gone wrong that she didn't about yet?

****

"All right. Keep me informed." Matt ended the call from the Critical Incident Response Group and immediately dialed Tuck. He wouldn't have answered his phone at all except a call from HQ meant it was important, and because he had nothing to do at the moment but drive himself insane with worry while Briar was having tests done.

"Hey, there's a situation escalating down in N.C. Former cop has taken his wife and two little girls hostage," he said when Tuck answered. "Negotiations have failed and the perp's gone silent. He's apparently got a psych history. Let the boys know they're on alert."

"Will do. You heading to HQ now?"

"No." He exhaled. "I'm at the hospital. Briar hemorrhaged a few hours ago."

"What?" Tuck said, shocked.

"I'm still waiting to hear what's going on. She's having tests done right now. Baby seems to be hanging in there so far, but we're not sure what's going to happen yet."

"Jesus. I'm sorry, is there anything I can do?"

Tuck was a prince of a guy, a former Delta operator who was steady under pressure, led the other guys by example. Matt was fortunate to have him serving as Blue Team's leader. "No, but thanks. Looks like you guys might have to do this one without me. Obviously I won't be able to deploy if things get critical." Replacing him as commander when they were looking at a tight timeline for deployment wasn't ideal. But what the hell choice did he have? "I can't leave her."

"Course not. Don't worry about anything else. I'll contact CIRG and keep you updated directly. You just look after your family."

The words hit Matt like an arrow in the chest. *My family.* A lump formed in his throat. He cleared it before speaking. "Thanks. I'll talk to you later." He checked the time, lowered the phone.

Briar still wasn't back yet. What the hell was taking so long?

Exhaling a deep breath, he leaned back in his seat and made one more call, for backup this time. Someone Briar would appreciate having around for extra support if they needed it. He would have called Taya but she had her own child to look after and Matt didn't want to bother her, especially when Schroder was being notified of a possible deployment right now.

Then it was back to waiting.

A few minutes later he glanced at his watch and shifted on the uncomfortable chair. How long did a fucking ultrasound take, anyway? When he'd come in with Briar for the ultrasound at nineteen weeks, they had been in and out of there within forty minutes. Yet here he'd been sitting in the hall for over ninety minutes this time.

It seemed to take forever until the elevator doors

opened and Briar finally rolled through on her bed. He jumped up from his chair and rushed over to her as they wheeled her down the hall. Her color was better, and she no longer had that pinched look on her face. "Hey. Everything okay?" he asked her, reaching for her hand.

She nodded, worry lurking in her dark eyes. "The doctor thinks my placenta may have torn a bit."

He nodded, having looked up some things before the call from CIRG. "So what does the doctor say that means for the baby?"

"She hasn't talked to me about the ultrasound results yet. The good news is, the bleeding's slowing. They think it's almost stopped. For now they want me on bed rest until they can guarantee there won't be more bleeding and the placenta moves away from my cervix."

Not the news he'd been hoping for. Not by a long shot. But better than he'd feared.

He continued with her into a room near the end of the hall. "I upgraded you to a private room," he said. At least one perk of his FBI health care coverage he could put to good use in this situation.

She let out a relieved sigh. "Thanks. Sharing a room with strangers right now when everything is up in the air would have made this a hundred times worse."

He nodded, moved out of the way while the nurse pushed the bed into position and put the brakes on. "Is the doctor going to come talk to us?"

"Yes," the nurse said. "I believe she's going over the ultrasound results with the radiologist right now." She paused to look at Briar. "Do you need anything at the moment?"

Briar shook her head. "No, I'm okay."

When the nurse left, the room got way too quiet. Matt pulled up a chair to the edge of the bed and sat in it before taking Briar's hand again. It was hard to see her being forced to lie so still. She was always active, always had something on the go. "How you holding up, honey?"

She turned her head, those liquid black eyes focusing on him. "I'm okay."

No she wasn't. How could she be when they didn't know if she or the baby were still in danger? But he didn't want to push, and he of all people understood why she felt the need for the strong, silent front she was putting on.

Just as quickly she looked away, began fiddling with the covers with her right hand. Betraying her anxiety in a way her expression and demeanor never would. "It might have been because of my flight yesterday."

She said it so softly he had to lean forward to catch it. "They told you that?"

"The doctor said she couldn't rule it out." She hesitated before continuing. "I had to fight to get her to sign off on allowing me to take the trip. What if… What if we lose the baby because of me?"

Matt's heart dropped. She was the most stubborn, independent woman he'd ever met. For her to admit that to him meant she must believe it was true, and that it was also weighing on her like an avalanche.

"Hey." He stood, leaned over her to cup her cheek. She blinked fast, but not fast enough to hide the sheen of moisture there. It cut him up inside, to see her this upset and blaming herself. "You can't do that to yourself. It wasn't your fault."

She swallowed and pressed her lips together, refused to look at him. "What if it was?" she said hoarsely. "How am I supposed to live with that if something happens to the baby?"

Ah, honey. He couldn't let her suffer through that kind of guilt and blame on top of everything else. "Come here," he murmured, sliding his arms around her back.

Briar grabbed onto him and turned her face into his neck, the strength of her grip and the fine tremors wracking her making him feel helpless. "I'm sorry," she whispered.

She thought he blamed her for this, he realized.

"No," he insisted with a shake of his head. "Nothing to be sorry for. All that matters now is making sure you and the baby are safe. Everything's gonna be fine." He'd been thinking about it a lot while she was getting her tests done. If she hemorrhaged again and for some reason he had to make a call between saving her life and the baby's, he wouldn't even have to think. Without hesitation he would tell them to save Briar.

She took several deep, shaky breaths, then slowly relaxed her grip on his shoulders and let go. Matt released her and straightened, smoothed her hair back from her forehead. She was so incredibly strong. Too strong, sometimes. It was hard for her to let herself lean on anyone, even him. He didn't ever want her to hesitate to lean on him if she needed him. "Let's just take this one step at a time together, okay?"

She nodded. Still wouldn't look at him.

Matt took her hand again just as the door opened and the doctor walked in. "Everything looks good with baby," she said with a smile.

Oh, thank God. Matt exhaled in acute relief and lowered himself into the chair, finally able to take a full breath for the first time since he'd seen all the blood on their bedroom floor. "Has the bleeding stopped?"

"For now it has. The placenta shows a slight tear close to the cervical os. As the third trimester progresses the placenta usually moves upward with the growth of the uterus, but for some reason it hasn't with your wife." The doctor looked at Briar. "I'd like to keep you in here for at least a week, to monitor the situation. We've got your blood typed and matched at the blood bank, just in case there's any more bleeding and we need to transfuse you."

"What would happen then?" Briar asked.

"If it's light, we'll keep you in here for further

observation. If it's heavy enough to jeopardize the baby's safety, then you might be looking at another transfusion or even an emergency C-section."

Briar put a hand to the mound of her belly and shot a worried look at Matt. "It's too early."

"But," the doctor added quickly, "in most cases the placenta will move away from the cervix in the coming weeks. Until that happens, you'll be on strict bed rest, whether it's here, or, if I feel it's safe for you, at home. It's too soon to talk about that right now, though, so in the meantime we'll keep checking to ensure the bleeding is stopped and make you as comfortable as we can. But as I said, baby is doing great."

"Okay," Briar said, and let out a deep breath, her face full of relief. "That's good news."

The doctor reached out to squeeze her shoulder. "Yes. Now I'm going to order you some supper and let you rest."

When the doc left Briar turned her head and gave him a weary smile. "I feel like I can finally breathe again."

"Me too," he agreed, and leaned over to kiss her gently. He was so damn grateful for the immediate danger to be over. "Love you."

She curled a hand behind his nape, squeezed. "Love you too."

After dinner a nurse came in to check Briar's pad and clean her up a bit. Matt stepped out into the hallway to give them some privacy, glanced up when he noticed rapid footsteps approaching him. He broke into a smile when he saw Trinity hurrying toward him. "Hey, glad you're here."

She didn't slow, a concerned frown stamped on her face. "What's happened? Is she okay? What about the baby?"

"They're okay for now." He brought her up to speed.

"Well thank God for that. What's going on down in

North Carolina?" she asked. "Brody just got called into HQ when I was on my way out."

Her fiancé Brody Colebrook, one of Matt's sniper team leaders. "Blue Team's being placed on alert."

She searched his eyes. "What about you? Are you going if they deploy?"

"I'm staying here. Don't say anything about the situation to Briar. She'll tell me to go now that everything seems to be calming down with her, and that's not happening."

"I won't."

"Thanks. Would you be able to swing by our place and pack her a bag later? She'll need some things if they're keeping her in here for a week."

"Of course, no problem."

"Thanks." He waited until the nurse exited Briar's room before holding the door for Trinity.

Lying flat on her back, Briar's face lit up when she saw her oldest friend. "What are you doing here?"

"Matt called me," she said, leaning over to hug Briar, then straightened to examine her. "You really okay?"

"Yes. Not gonna lie, though, that was scary as hell. I think we dodged a bullet."

"What's the latest sitrep?" Matt asked.

"No new bleeding, just a few small clots. We're still good."

Trinity put her hands on her hips, eyeing Briar. "So. Bed rest. As in, flat on your back bed rest until further notice. You're gonna do as you're told, right?"

Briar let out a grudging chuckle. "This time, yes." She rubbed her belly. "This little one's been through too much excitement already." She glanced at Matt, and he saw the remaining trace of guilt in her eyes.

Before he could say anything more to reassure her, his phone rang. He ignored it, but the women looked at him. "Sorry," he said, noticing as he pulled it out to silence it that the call was from the CIRG commander. He tucked it back into his pocket.

Briar lifted her eyebrows. "Something going on at work?"

"It's okay. Tuck's on it."

His wife stared at him for a long moment but let it go and resumed her visit with Trinity. When his phone buzzed twenty minutes later he pulled it out to find a text from Tuck.

Urgent. Call me or CIRG commander asap.

Hell. Matt glanced at Briar. "Be right back." He dialed Tuck as he stepped out into the hallway. "Hey. What's up?"

"Apparently you know the suspect."

Surprised, Matt headed for a quiet spot near the window at the far end of the hall. "I do?"

"The name Greg Harding ring a bell?"

Shock rippled through him as a face swam into focus in his mind. "Yeah. I met him back when I was first at the academy." Harding was a fellow Marine and had attached himself to Matt on the first day. "He washed out a month from graduation, wound up in psych care after he tried to kill himself." Matt had gone to see him, tried to get him the right help, but it hadn't been much and he could admit now that it hadn't been enough.

"He must have fooled everyone into thinking he was stable at some point, because he managed to became a cop."

Jesus, and now he'd snapped and taken his wife and kids hostage. "So what does CIRG want from me?" They knew about the situation with Briar.

"Harding initially told negotiators he'll talk to you."

Matt scrubbed a hand over his hair. Fuck. "Yeah, all right, I'll give it a shot. Have CIRG patch me through to the head negotiator."

Once he was on the line Matt told the negotiator what

he knew, agreed to speak to Harding over the phone if he was willing.

Fifteen minutes and multiple attempts to reach Harding later, the negotiator received a text. "*I'll only talk to DeLuca. In person*, it says."

Matt set his jaw. "I can't do that."

"Hang on, there's more. He says only you, and it has to be in person by tonight at seven or his family dies."

Shit. He dragged a hand over his face. What the hell did he do now? "Buy me some time. I have to think about this." Explain it to Briar, decide together what to do. "I'll call you back with an answer asap."

On his way back to Briar's room Matt thought of the little girls and their mother being held hostage by the man who was supposed to protect them. His gut clamped tight as a dark memory surfaced from an op he'd been on years ago, but he shoved it back in its box. Even though Briar was okay for now, he couldn't leave her.

Her keen gaze locked on him when he pushed the door open. "What's happening?"

He let it swing shut behind him. "Domestic dispute became an armed hostage situation in North Carolina. Marine vet threatening to kill his wife and kids."

"Is one of your teams responding?"

He nodded. "Blue Team's being deployed."

"With who as commander?"

"Not sure. Maybe Grant." Gold Team's leader. He had the training and experience. He could handle it.

Briar looked at Trinity. "You knew."

Trinity didn't deny it. "Brody got called in just as I was leaving."

Briar turned her attention back to him, a tiny bit of annoyance in her gaze that they had hidden it from her.

Matt blew out a breath. "There's more." He told her about Harding and their history. "He says he'll only talk to me, and only in person. I've got until seven tonight to make it happen, or he kills his wife and little girls."

Briar didn't hesitate. "You should go."

His spine straightened. *To hell.* "My place is here with you."

"No. You heard the doctor. I'm fine. Baby's fine. There's nothing more you can do for either of us, but you might be able to save that woman and her daughters."

"I can't leave you like this."

Her expression softened. "I love that you want to be here for me, but I'm okay. You might be the only person who can stop this from getting any uglier. You have to go."

He shook his head, opened his mouth to refuse again but Trinity cut him off.

"I'll stay with her," she offered.

Briar smiled, patted her friend's hand. "See? She'll stay with me."

"I'm in between jobs right now," Trinity went on. "Got nothing better to do, and if Brody's going with you—" As if on cue her cell chimed. She pulled it out, gave a rueful smile. "Speak of the devil. Okay, he's definitely going. So I'll stay here and camp out with our girl, make sure she behaves herself," she said with a warning look at Briar, "and as soon as everything wraps up you can come straight back here."

"I'll be good, I promise," Briar said, looking from him to Trinity and back again. "You know you have to go. You won't be able to live with yourself if you don't and it all goes wrong."

"I won't be able to live with myself if I leave and anything happens to *you*," he argued. But she was right. If she and the baby weren't in immediate danger and they were only keeping her in for observation, and if Trin stayed with her... He would be an hour flight away. Hopefully he would be able to make contact with Harding and resolve this within a couple hours. And if he could save the wife and little girls, the duty bound part of him felt obligated to go.

"Are you *sure*?" he asked. Because he wasn't.

"I'm positive," Briar said. "I'm telling you, go. It's okay. I love you and I'll be right here waiting when you get back." She grabbed for his hand, squeezed it. "Just be careful and don't take any stupid risks."

Matt was so damn torn. He weighed the decision in his mind, glanced between the two women. When they both nodded at him in encouragement, he relented.

"All right. But I'm keeping my cell on me at all times. If anything happens, and I mean *anything*," he said with a hard look at them both, "any more bleeding, another big clot, whatever, Trinity calls me immediately and I'll be back here as fast as I can. Got it?"

The women nodded. "Got it," they echoed, their expressions almost identical. It was eerie, how they did that.

His gaze slid to his wife, his conscience needling him. Shit, he didn't want to go. His job required a lot of sacrifices on his behalf, but he'd never been this torn between duty and family before.

As if reading his thoughts, Briar's lips curved into a knowing smile as she reached up to cup the side of his face. "Go make the world a better place." She gave his shoulder a little push. "Go."

"All right, I'm going," he grumbled. "Love you," he added, then bent to kiss her. Straightening, he pointed a finger at Trinity. "You hold her to her promise. Don't let her move until I get back."

"Oh, I won't. She's never had a warden this tough."

Since that was the best assurance he could get under the circumstances, Matt made himself walk out the door and call the negotiator. "I'm on my way," Matt told the man as he strode for the elevator. "Have everything ready when I get there."

Chapter Six

"You really okay, or are you just faking it?" Trinity asked her after Matt left. "Because if you're faking it in front of me, I'm gonna be pissed."

Briar wanted Matt here, but in light of the circumstances, had pushed him to do the right thing. "I'm good. Just glad everything's okay with the baby. That was scary." Briar put a hand to her belly. Was it her imagination, or did the baby's movements seem weaker and less frequent than they had yesterday? "I still feel guilty, though."

She told Trin about the flying bit. "Matt and I had a fight about it before I left on this last trip. He thought it was too risky this late and was mad I went to the doctor and got permission to go anyway. In this case, turns out he was right," she muttered.

"Yeah, and I know how much we both hate having to admit we're wrong," Trin said wryly.

Briar gave a half smile. She felt better about the baby now, but if something else went wrong and they lost it, part of her wondered if Matt would secretly blame her for it. She didn't think she could handle that.

Trin took her hand. "You only think that because deep down where no one else can see, you and I are neurotic nutjobs. The doctor said she couldn't be sure whether this was partly due to the flight or not. Matt told me it could have been caused by a bunch of different things, so if you're quietly worrying that he's upset with you, he's not. He's a smart guy."

"Who's already lost a wife and child," Briar pointed out.

"I know. But he's not going to lose you guys." She laid a hand on Briar's belly, a startled look coming over her face when the baby either kicked or punched. Briar had often sensed that her friend had wanted to touch her belly, but Trinity hadn't until now. "What does it feel like?" Trin asked, her expression full of wonder.

Briar's heart ached for her friend. About a year ago Trin had confessed that she would have loved to have a baby, and she had more maternal instincts in her little finger than Briar did in her whole body. The Valkyrie Program had taken many things from Trin, but it hadn't been able to destroy that part of her soul. "At first it was like tiny little bubbles fizzing around inside. Then tiny bumps and rolls that kept growing stronger. It felt weird at first but now I love it." And she was extra glad to feel the baby moving now. It reassured her.

Trin nodded, gaze glued to her hand, perfectly manicured fingers splayed across Briar's belly. "It must be so amazing, knowing you have a little being tucked away inside you."

It really was.

Briar was quiet a moment. "Have you and Brody ever thought about maybe adopting one day?"

Trin removed her hand and sat back, her expression neutral. "We haven't really talked about having a family."

"Why not? You love kids, and I thought you said he

did too."

She lifted a shoulder, her inky hair swaying with the movement. Her friend was every bit as beautiful on the inside as her gorgeous exterior. She deserved to be a mother to some lucky child out there who needed a good home. "I don't want to get ahead of myself. It took me forever to agree to a wedding date. One step at a time."

Briar decided not to push, because she understood. "I get it. It's hard for us to undo what was done to us."

She nodded. "Feels impossible sometimes, doesn't it? It's a two steps forward, one step back kinda deal. Though having an amazing partner makes it a lot easier."

"True." She could count on Matt, no matter what. Briar sighed. Life wasn't fair. Trin shouldn't have had the choice to have children taken from her. Just as Matt shouldn't have lost Lisa and their baby, or feel responsible if he couldn't save the hostages today.

"What's wrong?"

"Nothing." She rubbed her belly. *You okay in there, little one? We have to get through this together.*

"Lemme guess. You're still blaming yourself for this and determined to continue blaming yourself no matter what anyone else says," Trin finished in exasperation.

She wasn't wrong. But there was more. "Do you ever feel like something's...missing inside us?"

She gave Briar a bland look. "You'll have to be more specific."

Briar chuckled at her friend's dark, dry humor. She hadn't been referring to Trinity's hysterectomy. "I worded that badly. I mean emotionally."

Trin frowned. "What do you mean?"

"You know." She lifted a shoulder. "The softness part. The—" She cringed inside. "Feelings."

"Ah. Yeah, all the time. Not surprising, given what they did to us."

Briar had been much younger than Trinity when she'd

entered the program. She hadn't seen it as a bad thing at the time. On the contrary, she'd thought it was awesome and empowering, learning to conceal emotion and being trained in all kinds of cool things. Tactics, self-defense, survival skills, weapons. How to infiltrate a position, make a kill and get out without leaving a trace. It had given her a purpose and something to focus on other than her pain, the grief that had threatened to destroy her.

Looking at Trin now, she pushed aside the guilt and horrible sense of vulnerability at saying the rest of it aloud. Trin understood her better than anyone ever could, even Matt. They were weapons. Trained killers. Not exactly the qualifications necessary to take care of and raise children.

"What if I'm not mother material?" she said. "What if I've made this really selfish decision to have a baby, and it turns out I'm a shitty parent?"

Trin shook her head. "Not gonna happen. And there's no such thing as a perfect parent anyway. Believe me, there are *way* shittier parents out there than you could ever be, my own included." She tilted her head, considering her. "What's brought this on?"

Briar shrugged as if it was no big deal, when in reality these nagging little doubts had been growing louder in her head over the past few months. "Just some things that have been bothering me for a while."

"Such as?"

Things she wouldn't dare breathe a word about to anyone except for Trinity. "Well, Matt for instance. There's been a lot of friction between us about my job lately. Then a couple weeks ago he was cleaning out some boxes in his office and I found some pictures of him and Lisa lying on his desk that he hadn't put away."

That had hurt. Logically she knew it was stupid to feel that way, but there it was. She might put on the tough act for the rest of the world because that's what she wanted everyone to see, but there were still insecurities lurking deep inside her.

"She was a big part of his life long before you came along. It's normal for him to still think of her and have pictures of her. It's not like he's pining for her, or that he wishes he still had her instead of you."

"You should hear how he talks about her, though. She doesn't come up often, but when she does he gets this...faraway look in his eyes and this smile on his face." Briar wasn't proud to admit that it made her jealous. "She was like a human sunbeam. Warm, funny, sweet, always wanted to be a mother, loved his family. The perfect wife. I bet she never argued with him." She glanced at Trinity. "I'm none of those things." She was Lisa's polar opposite.

Trin stared at her in clear surprise. "Wait. Are you seriously feeling insecure about your relationship with Matt?"

Briar looked away. "I know he loves me. But he's the kind of guy to stick with me now no matter what, even if he's unhappy."

"Sweetie, he's not unhappy."

He'd never come out and said it, but he'd sure seemed unhappy with her a lot these past few months because of her refusal to stop doing certain things. "I dunno. Sometimes I wonder if he was way happier with her than he is with me. That maybe they were a better fit."

"Okay, I'm going to go ahead and blame all this on pregnancy hormones and a shitload of stress. Are you kidding me? Yes, he loved her. But I guarantee she wasn't perfect. Who is? And yeah, to you she might seem like the perfect homemaker who couldn't wait to have a dozen babies and do the stay at home mom thing, but could she handle a weapon like you? No. Could she take out a target with a headshot from a thousand meters?" Trin raised her eyebrows in silent demand. "Or go off grid behind enemy lines alone for weeks at a time to take out a target? I don't think so."

Briar huffed out a laugh. The comparisons sounded twice as ridiculous out loud. "That's not even apples and oranges it's so far out there."

"Well, Matt thinks your apples are sexy as hell, and I have to agree. Come on, you know how much he loves it that you can shoot as well as he can. *Hot*."

"I shoot better than him." She grinned, watched her friend settle back into the chair. "I love you, you know."

Trin smiled. "Back atcha. And see? There's the softness and feelings you were so worried about not having. Know what else? You would never have said that to me until about two years ago unless under torture. And you also haven't stopped stroking your belly since I walked in. You love this baby, and would do anything to protect it."

She reached out, snagged Briar's hand and squeezed, her deep blue eyes full of a fierce love that warmed Briar inside and out. "Everything's gonna be fine. There's nothing missing inside you, it's just that bits might be...dormant. And I'll always be here for you, no matter what."

"Ditto." Valkyries for life. An unbreakable bond a hundred times stronger than blood.

An unintended positive side effect that Briar would bet their handlers had never anticipated.

****

Matt was surprised when Harding picked up the phone when he called the number. "Greg. It's Matt DeLuca. I got down here as soon as I could. Want to tell me what's going on?"

Everyone in the mobile command center was staring at him. Tuck stood off in the far corner, the rest of Blue Team waiting outside. They were parked a block from the target house. Outside, it was getting dark already. The entire neighborhood was locked down, swarming with cops and FBI agents.

"It's too late," Harding said in misery. "It's no good."

"It's not too late," Matt said, watching the chief negotiator, who was analyzing every word they spoke.

Harding was becoming increasingly unstable and it seemed to be accelerating. He was on at least six different psychiatric meds, and no one knew if he'd simply stopped taking them or if something else had gone wrong. Over the past few months his mental state and marriage had deteriorated, to the point where the wife had finally decided to leave him and take the children with her.

Matt tried again. "I came all the way down here because you asked for me. Let me help."

The negotiator nodded at him, made a circling motion with his hand to keep going.

"Sherry's gonna leave me. She swears she won't now but I know she's lying." A muffled sob came through the line. "She's gonna fucking leave me after all we've been through together, and take the girls with her. She's got somebody else, I know it. My life's over."

Matt's number one priority was getting the wife and kids out unharmed. Doing the same for Harding was a distant second, history between them or not. "It's not over, Greg, and we're here to help. Do the right thing, let Sherry and the girls go, then come out and give yourself up so we can talk."

Harding let out a bitter laugh. "You think I'm that stupid? That it's that easy? You had the chance to help me years ago and you fucking walked away, left me to deal with everything on my own. We were friends, I thought I could count on you, and then you cut me out of your life."

Matt clenched his jaw and waited a beat. He wasn't responsible for Harding's actions. And they'd never been friends. "Let them go, Greg, then come out and we'll talk."

"I don't think so."

It was like a switch had flipped in the guy's brain. Matt looked at Tuck, the evil edge to Harding's voice making the back of his neck tingle. Tuck nodded and jumped out the door to get the team in place for an assault.

"Greg. Listen to me. I can help you."

"No, you listen to *me*. You think you're a hero for making the sacrifice to show up here to save the day? That you're the original American badass because you were a Scout/Sniper and went on to become the HRT commander? Well I know the truth."

He didn't like the ominous tone or the direction this was headed. As far as sacrifice, yeah, he'd made a big one in coming down here for this, leaving his wife and unborn child at an uncertain time.

He'd called Briar when he landed at the local airport several hours ago, and everything was still good with her. No more bleeding, baby's heartbeat was strong. It took a huge load off his shoulders to be able to put that aside for the moment and concentrate solely on the incident at hand.

"What truth?" he said, needing to keep Harding talking.

An oily, malicious chuckle answered. "I know what happened on the op in Khost."

Matt stilled in surprise, that day flooding back in a rush. It should still be classified. How did Harding know about it?

"Yeah, I know what happened with that warlord and the kids he had as hostages. I was on patrol in the city and heard all about it." He paused. "You couldn't save them. I bet that still bothers you, doesn't it? Yeah, it would drive you fucking nuts." Another chuckle.

Matt's fingers tightened around the phone. He pushed aside his personal feelings for this asshole and attempted again to be the voice of reason. "Greg. I need you to let your family go and come out with your hands up."

"I don't think so. You couldn't save those kids that day. And you know what? Nothing's changed. Because even if you did make it all the way to commander of the HRT, you'll never be a hero. Not to me."

Matt was losing him. He didn't know what the hell else to stay to stall for more time. "Greg—"

"You didn't save those girls then. You had your shot to do something about it, and you didn't. Just like you did with me. And guess what? You won't save my girls today either."

The line went dead.

Fuck. Matt immediately called him back as the mobile command center erupted into noise and motion.

Harding didn't answer.

Matt spun to face the negotiator. "Keep trying him." He stood before the bank of monitors and slipped his earpiece in so he could hear what the team was saying as they moved into position for the breach. "Tuck, he cut contact. You gotta get in there right now."

"Understood. Stand by."

Matt thought about Harding's young girls. He had seen pictures of them on the flight down here. Seven and five years old, both blond with big brown eyes. He couldn't get their faces out of his head.

Though he tried to ignore Harding's words, they conjured up old memories as he waited, pushing against the mental barrier he'd put up. Of a time in Afghanistan when he and his spotter had been watching a wanted Taliban warlord. Two little girls had been caught up in a bad situation when the warlord had discovered he was cornered and taken five hostages to shield himself from air strikes.

Matt had the bastard in the center of his crosshairs twice, but each time rules of engagement prevented him from taking the shot that could have rid the world of another terrorist and saved innocent lives. Instead, all the hostages had died, including those two little girls before he'd finally been given clearance to take the shot.

Matt had put a 7.62 round through the back of the bastard's head a heartbeat later, but it hadn't erased the guilt he still carried to this day. He and his spotter had been forced to stay in their hide and watch as the lifeless bodies were carried out. Like limp ragdolls over the villagers' shoulders before they were dumped unceremoniously on the ground to lie there until their frantic parents arrived on scene.

Harding was right. He hadn't done everything he could to save those girls.

But he and his team were damn well going to save these ones today.

"Sitrep," he said to Tuck.

"In position. Stand by."

Pop, pop.

Matt's head snapped up. "Shots fired." A pistol. *Fuck.* He glanced at the other screens in front of him, which told him nothing. "*Go*," he told Tuck.

Tuck gave the signal for the assault.

Matt was totally focused on the footage on the screen as the team stormed the side entrance and rushed into the basement. More shots exploded. Matt set his jaw, stood rock still as he followed the team's progress.

Evers reached the locked door in the basement. Matt could clearly hear cries of pain in the background. High-pitched and terrified. From a child.

Get them out. Get them out, he willed his guys. He watched the footage intently, every muscle in his body drawn tight.

Harding had rigged an IED on the lock. It took Bauer and Tuck precious minutes to disable it and let Evers ram the door. It was barricaded from the inside. They had to climb over furniture on the way inside.

Tuck's helmet cam gave Matt a perfect view of the spare bedroom, its window covered with a quilt to prevent anyone from seeing inside.

Bodies. On the floor beside a bed. The cries were louder now, turning into sobs. Someone moved just out of view on the far side of the bed.

The team secured the room. "Suspect down," Tuck reported. "Two wounded."

But not dead. Not yet. "Clear to send the EMTs in?"

"Yes."

Matt signaled to one of his subordinates. "On the double."

"Suspect's dead," Schroder reported a moment later. "Wife and one daughter wounded. Wife is critical."

"Bringing the girls out now." Bauer. "Youngest appears uninjured. Older one has GSW to the thigh."

Matt curled his hands into fists where they rested beneath his armpits. "Copy that. EMTs coming to you." He headed out of the command center and jogged the block to the target house.

Bauer was coming toward him, a little girl cradled in his arms. He reached the sidewalk where the ambulance was moving into position and set her down on the grass, a bandage wrapped around her thigh. Blackwell appeared carrying her sister a moment later. The little girl was huddled against his chest, her thin arms wrapped tight around his neck, her face pressed into his shoulder.

Matt's heart ached at the sight. Bauer and Blackwell were both daddies, and he was about to be. Seeing kids suffering or dying was the hardest part of this job. It never got any easier, and it never went away. Matt wished Harding was still alive so he could punch him repeatedly in the face. How could a father fucking do something like this?

Matt crouched down next to the wounded girl while

Bauer adjusted the bandage. "Hi, Amy. I'm Matt."

Her big brown eyes darted to him, wide with shock, her skin chalky. Her teeth chattered, her whole body trembling.

Matt reached for her hand, wrapped his fingers around her icy cold ones. "You're safe now. These men are going to look at your leg and make you feel better, okay?" he said, nodding at the approaching paramedics. "And look, here's your sister."

Amy let out a sob and cranked her head around just as Blackwell knelt down beside her. Erin raised her tearstained face and burst into tears when she saw Amy, reaching for her older sister. "I want my mom," she cried, glancing around frantically for her. "She's hurt real b-bad."

"People are looking after her right now," Blackwell said, stroking the girl's trembling back. "They're going to take her to the hospital where the doctors can help her."

"D-daddy sh-shot at us," the girl sobbed. "He was hurt t-too."

Matt shared a look with his guys. These two girls would forever be scarred by what had happened today, but at least they were alive.

He and the others moved back as the paramedics took over. "How's the mother look?" Matt asked when they were out of earshot.

"Two bullets center mass. Fucking coward shot her and the older girl, then blew his own head off when he heard us coming."

Schroder was coming across the lawn, peeling off his latex gloves, the others behind him. "Girls okay?" he asked in concern, looking over where the paramedics and victim assistance personnel were with them.

"As well as can be expected," Matt said. "I just hope their mom makes it." After going through this, they were going to need the love and support of a parent more than ever.

"Doesn't look good," Schroder said, his face grim. Then he looked at Matt. "How about you? We heard what he said."

"I'm good." Pissed as hell at Harding, and yeah, a little shaken at how close these girls had come to dying. But mostly he just wanted to get this wrapped up as fast as possible so he could get back to his wife and baby.

Chapter Seven

"I wish they'd stop pumping me full of fluids," Briar grumbled as she rolled slightly to reach for the call button. This was the fourth time she'd had to relieve herself since lunch. "I've got no place to put them anymore."

Trinity chuckled from the pullout chair next to the bed and set her e-reader down. "I really do love you, but I don't want to help you with your bedpan."

"I don't want you to either. Gross." She settled back into position, not quite flat on her back, turned slightly onto her left side to help alleviate the pressure of the baby on her aorta. This bed rest thing already wasn't fun. She had to mentally gear up for the coming weeks ahead of her. "What time is it, anyway?" She reached for her phone on the side table.

"Almost seven. At night," Trinity added.

Briar shot her a wry look. "Thanks for the clarification."

She'd heard nothing more from Matt since he'd called from the airport in North Carolina hours before. Things obviously hadn't been resolved peacefully yet. Had they rescued the girls and their mother? She looked up a few news network sites she mostly trusted but the only story she could find about it said merely that there was a hostage situation happening at a home in a residential neighborhood.

A nurse entered the room. "Hi there," she said, giving Briar a big smile.

"Hi. I need to use the bedpan again."

"And that's my cue to leave," Trinity said, getting to her feet and taking her e-reader with her. "Good luck. Aim well."

Briar shook her head as her friend left. The nurse got the bedpan and positioned herself near Briar's hip. "Okay, lift up," she instructed.

Briar's face heated. "Can I have a little privacy for this?"

"Of course, once I make sure you're all lined up." She shifted the cold pan under Briar's rear, then stepped back and pulled the curtain around the side of the bed. "All right. Shoot."

Briar snorted. "You're as bad as my friend." It was hard not to feel a little self-conscious with someone standing two feet away listening in while she did her business, but she managed. "Can I get a washcloth to clean up with? Please," she added. Turned out her "aim" with bedpans was pretty much a total fail compared to with a rifle.

"Sure." The water ran in the sink, then the nurse pulled the curtain back and handed the cloth to her.

Briar pushed aside the squirming discomfort at what was coming. The worst part was *after* using the bedpan, because the nurses had to check the contents to make sure there was no bleeding. There was no dignity right now, and wouldn't be for the foreseeable future.

Briar obediently lifted her hips so the nurse could slide the pan out from under her, and one look at her face when the woman looked into the pan made Briar's heart stutter. "What's wrong?" She craned her neck, trying to see for herself.

Blood. Bright red blood. As much as there had been that morning. Maybe more.

A wave of ice rushed through her body.

"I'm going to get the doctor on call," the nurse said, and rushed out, leaving Briar there with her heart in her throat as she stared at the blood.

No. No, come on, stop…

She swallowed, willed her pulse to slow while she waited, her hand on her belly. She could feel something warm spilling from inside her. A slow trickle. "Come on, damn you. *Stop*," she hissed at her body.

Her mind raced, fear threatening to take over. The baby wasn't moving right now. Hadn't been active over the past couple of hours.

Trinity came back in. "Everything okay? The nurse looked like she was in a hurry."

"I'm bleeding again," she said, fighting to stay calm.

Face full of concern, Trinity came to stand at the side of the bed, looking at the mattress. "I'll get you a towel to clean up with."

Just as she turned back with it, Briar felt a warm gush between her legs. "Oh, shit," she breathed. Trinity froze, her gaze locked on the sheet turning red beneath Briar.

"Don't move. I'll get someone," Trinity said, and rushed out.

Briar pressed the towel between her legs, tried to elevate her hips. Her heartbeat thudded in her ears. *No, no, no.* Not again.

The towel was already half-soaked by the time anyone came back in. There was no suppressing the fear now. She was bleeding way heavier than she had last night.

Four nurses came in, an unfamiliar female doctor right behind them. One of the nurses put the Doppler on Briar's belly while another strapped her up to some kind of monitor.

The doctor moved into position next to the bed, watching the monitor as the feed began. "Alert the blood bank," she said to no one in particular, listening to the Doppler. A nurse hurried out of the room.

The nurse moved the device over Briar's belly, trying to locate the heartbeat. A quiet whooshing sound made Briar close her eyes in relief. The heartbeat was still there. But when she opened her eyes the doctor looked grim.

"Has baby been moving much lately?" she asked Briar.

"No." She looked at the monitor, fought back the cold wave of panic that threatened to swamp her. Was it her imagination, or did the heartbeat seem weaker? Sluggish almost?

The doctor issued orders to the nurses, who moved with fast efficiency to do her bidding. Briar didn't understand most of what they were saying, but she caught the gist and it confirmed what she feared most.

This was really bad.

"Is the baby okay?" Briar demanded, struggling to remain calm inside.

"It's in distress," the doctor answered. "Right now the heart rate is dangerously low."

The bottom of Briar's stomach dropped out. *Oh my God. Oh my God, no.* "Can you do anything to fix it?"

"If the heart rate doesn't come back up in the next few minutes, we're going to have to get you into an operating room and get the baby out."

Briar stared at her. She had known since last night that this was a possibility. But she wasn't ready for it. Not yet. And not without Matt here.

As good as she was at suppressing emotion, this was too much. Her throat thickened, tears burning the backs of her eyes. *It's too soon.*

A minute later the doctor looked at one of the nurses who was changing the towel between Briar's legs. "Is it slowing?"

"No."

Briar held her breath, waiting along with the doctor as they watched the monitor and listened to the heartbeat. Too slow. Too damn slow. And she was losing a scary amount of blood. The baby's oxygen supply continued to flow out of her with every beat of her heart.

The doctor finally shook her head. "Prep the OR and have the anesthetist start a spinal. Go."

Her words echoed in Briar's head, sounding far away. *I can't have the baby yet. I just can't.*

As people rushed out she took Briar's hand, squeezed it. "I don't want to wait. I'd rather get your baby out and into the NICU than risk losing it."

This was a nightmare. It was way too soon. Were the baby's lungs going to be developed enough? But since there was no other choice Briar nodded, not trusting her voice for a moment.

She struggled to find the words, keep her voice from shaking. "My husband is at work." He'd said he would keep his phone on him, but if the team had to go in after the suspect to save the hostages, he couldn't just answer.

"Your friend is outside. Can she call him?"

"Yes." Of course. Trinity would handle it.

The doctor squeezed her hand once more and let go, giving Briar a reassuring smile. "I'm going to scrub in. I'll see you down in the OR in a few minutes."

After the woman left, Briar squeezed her eyes shut and fought to breathe, pressing both hands to her belly. She willed her baby to move. To fight.

Her body was failing her child. Only medical technology could save it now.

The burn at the back of her throat and eyes intensified but she swallowed back the tears threatening to erupt.

Crying was for the weak. Right now she had to stay calm and be the warrior her baby needed—the one she'd been trained to be.

Even so, she couldn't help but send out a silent plea. *Hold on, little one. Please hold on.*

****

In the back of the FBI Blackhawk, Matt snatched his phone from his pocket when it vibrated against his hip. Seeing Trinity's number, his blood pressure plummeted.

Shoving the earphones off, he plugged one finger into his ear as he pressed the phone to the other. "Trinity. Everything okay?" But she wouldn't be calling if it were.

She said something he didn't catch over the sound of the engines and the pulse of the rotors.

"Can't hear you. Text me," he said over the noise in the cabin. He lowered the phone and waited, staring anxiously at the screen. A moment later a text appeared.

She's bleeding again. Worse this time.

"Aw, *shit*." He started to type out a response, only got the first two words done when another message popped up.

They're taking her down to the OR for an emergency C-section.

Jesus Christ. The blood drained from his face, his heart knocking against his ribs. *How soon?*

On her way now.

He was stuck in the air. God, he had to get to her in time. *I'm on my way.*

Will stay with her until you get here.

Phone in hand, he got up and signaled the crew chief for his headset while the guys all watched him in concern. Matt put it on and spoke to the pilots. "My wife's being rushed in for an emergency C-section. I need you to drop me off on the hospital roof." He gave the name and location of it. "Clear it with whoever you need to, use my authorization. Just get me there before the baby's born."

"You got it," one of them replied.

"How far out are we?"

"Eighteen to twenty minutes."

A long fucking time to wait when the lives of his wife and child were at risk. But this was the best he could do.

When Matt turned around his team members were all staring at him. He slipped his other headset back on and hit the toggle on the cord to talk to them. "Change of plans. Briar hemorrhaged and she's being prepped for surgery."

Shock flickered on their faces.

"Pilots are dropping me at the hospital and then flying you guys to base."

Tuck responded. "Anything you need, brother."

Bauer nodded and gave him a thumbs up. "Hang in there. Briar's tough and babies are a lot stronger than they look."

Matt nodded his thanks and sat his ass back down to wait. He didn't want to talk, frantic to get to his wife in time.

This was all wrong, was happening too fast. He'd looked it up while he was waiting for Briar to have all her tests done. The baby was way too young to be born yet. The chances of complications or severe problems were high. He'd read things like brain damage, organ failure. Fuck, it was heartbreaking.

ETA 20 mins he sent to Trinity. Tuck reached over to tap his knee. Matt looked up but his phone vibrated again. The blood pulsed in his ears as he read the text.

Doctor can't wait. Needs to get baby out.

Of course, whatever they needed to do. *Understood.*

Trinity sent back a thumbs up. *In waiting room. They're putting in a spinal now.*

How is she? Matt asked. She must be fucking terrified,

although she would never show or admit it. God dammit, he needed to be there. Needed to hold her, at least her hand, and stand beside her through this so she didn't have to go through it alone.

Strong.

The one word answer set off a bittersweet pang inside him. Briar *was* strong. The strongest woman he had ever known. And she would fight with everything in her to get through this, protect their baby any way she could.

Be there asap, he typed. *Tell her I'm coming.*

Will pass it on. Hang in there.

He didn't have a choice, did he?

The minutes passed by with agonizing slowness. He kept checking his watch, phone in hand so he would get Trinity's texts the moment she sent an update.

The crew chief flagged him down. Matt started to take his headphones off but the guy held up his hand, fingers outspread, and pointed at the floor.

Five minutes.

Matt nodded, his stomach in knots, willing the helo to go faster. As soon as they began their descent he ripped off his headset and moved toward the crew chief over by the starboard door.

He peered through the windows as they descended through the clouds. The lights of the darkened city finally appeared.

As they moved lower, Matt spotted the hospital and the landing pad on top of the roof. It was empty, saving him the trouble of having to fast rope out of the helo. Which he totally had been prepared to do if the pilots couldn't land.

His heart beat faster as the pilots came in to land, lowering into a hover above the large red H marked on the concrete. The instant the wheels touched, the crew chief threw the door open. "Good luck," he shouted, slapping Matt on the back.

He didn't even look back at his team as he jumped out and ran for the door marking the top of the stairwell, realized only belatedly when a hand reached out to jerk the door open for him that Tuck had hopped out with him.

Matt looked at him as the rotor wash from the helo beat against their bodies, nodded once in silent thank you before he turned and ran down the darkened stairwell. He needed to get into the OR in time to be there for his wife and see their baby born.

Chapter Eight

The operating room was freezing, but it didn't come close to the arctic level of cold inside her.

Briar shivered as she lay on her side, a pad wedged between her thighs to absorb the blood still coming out of her as the anesthetist pushed the needle into her lower back. She used the bite of pain to center her, push back the building wall of emotion that grew higher with each passing minute.

"Okay, spinal's in," he announced.

The door swung open and the female doctor walked in dressed in scrubs, a surgical mask loose around her neck. "Your friend said to tell you she contacted your husband. He's on the way."

For some reason that pushed her precariously close to losing the fight against the tears scalding the backs of her eyes. She could do this alone but she would much rather have Matt here. "Where is he now?"

"I'm not sure." She glanced at the anesthetist, gave Briar a smile. "Almost ready. Let's get this baby born."

It had been less than a minute since the spinal went in but already her lower body was numb and unresponsive when she tried to move. A weird, unsettling feeling. She hated feeling trapped and helpless, and right now she was both.

The team positioned her on her back and began putting up the privacy barrier across her middle that would hide the procedure from her view. She didn't mind blood and guts, but didn't want to see her own as they operated.

As she lay there, the numbness in her lower body seemed to creep higher, reaching her lungs. All of a sudden it was harder to breathe.

A burst of panic flashed through her. "I can't breathe," she blurted out, breaking into a cold sweat. She couldn't move. Couldn't get enough air.

"The sensation you're feeling is normal," the anesthetist said behind her. "Just try to relax and keep breathing."

Relax? Was he fucking kidding right now? Her baby's life was in danger and she couldn't do a damn thing about it.

But she did as he said, struggling through each breath, hating every second of this yet more terrified that her baby wouldn't make it. Or that it wouldn't survive long after being born.

That was too horrible to think about. She didn't know what she would do if the baby died, and Matt… He would be leveled.

She wished he were here. Trinity had offered to come in with her during the operation and the doctor would have allowed it but Briar didn't want anyone except her husband and if he couldn't be here then she would do this alone.

The slow blip of the baby's heartbeat beeped in the background. It seemed even slower than it had a few minutes ago.

Hurry, she urged them, battling the inclination to snap it. She was numb from the chest down. She just wanted the baby out so they could help it.

"All right, Briar. Can you feel this?" The doctor had her mask on now, a surgical shield over her face as she looked at Briar over the top of the blue curtain. A team of nurses stood by, ready to assist and whisk the baby off to the NICU once it was born.

Briar shook her head, unable to feel a thing but the heaviness in her lungs and the fear eating through her carefully constructed control. Each breath was an effort, like she had to force her lungs to inflate every time she inhaled. The shock made everything worse.

In a few minutes, she was going to be a mother. It was so hard to wrap her mind around that, or to move past the fear of what she would do if something was wrong with the baby.

"Okay, then we're ready," the doctor said.

Briar braced herself for what was coming, closed her eyes. *Almost over. Stay calm. You can do this. Just please let the baby be all right.*

Nausea welled up out of nowhere. She opened her eyes. Swallowed repeatedly, willing the sensation to pass, and clenched her teeth to keep them from chattering while she worked to breathe. Everything about this was worse than she had imagined.

Motion to the right caught her eye. She turned her head in time to see another nurse push the OR door open. "Hang on, we've got a last minute addition to our group," she said, smiling at Briar.

Hope exploded inside her. Her heart stuttered, and when Matt appeared in the doorway dressed in scrubs and a hair net, she almost gave into the need to burst into tears.

He strode straight to her, his face filled with concern. "Hey, sweetheart." He bent and kissed her softly, gripped both of her hands in his warm ones when she reached up to him. Then he gave her a smile. "I made it."

The jagged edge of fear receded. She couldn't answer,

her chest and throat were too tight. Instead she pulled his hands to her mouth and held them there, grateful to be able to have him here as her anchor. The cold and apprehension were still there but now they were bearable with him beside her.

"Here you go, dad," a nurse said, sliding a chair in behind him.

Matt tugged his mask into place over his mouth and nose and sat behind Briar's head, joined their hands and resting them on her chest. Somehow he made it seem easier to breathe. She'd been so damn scared until he'd walked in and now she didn't have to carry the load alone.

"It's gonna be okay," he told her softly, rubbing his thumbs over the backs of her knuckles. Calm. Steady as ever.

"I've made the first incision," the doctor announced from the other side of the low curtain. "You doing all right?"

"Mmhmm," Briar managed, her jaw still shaking a little from shock and cold. It felt like her whole body was quivering.

"Good. Now you're going to feel some pressure."

A dozen different emotions all churned inside her. She was still afraid for the baby, but there was also hope and excitement and shock.

She tensed when she felt the pressure on her stomach. It was strange because she couldn't feel any pain, and knowing she was lying there cut open like a fish was unsettling in its own sense.

"All right, now some tugging. Just keep breathing, you're doing great."

Briar looked up at her husband. Matt met her gaze, his clear green eyes visible above the edge of the surgical mask.

Calm. Solid. She drew strength from him, calmed her heart rate. Matt wouldn't let anything happen to her and the baby. The thought wasn't logical but she didn't care. She absolutely trusted him to ensure her safety.

"So, are you two ready to meet your baby?" the doctor said a minute later.

Briar held her breath, her heart thudding hard against her ribs. She dug her fingers into Matt's hands, felt him squeeze tight. *Yes. Yes, I'm ready.*

"Suction."

A sucking sound filled the room. More tugs, more pressure.

"And…it's a girl."

The words pinged through Briar's mind like a ricochet. A girl? She'd been convinced it was a boy, but ohhh…

I have a daughter.

A tiny, thin cry split the quiet. The sound of it twisted her heart, her brain instantly recognizing it as her child. Briar jerked her head up off the table, her gaze locked on the partition blocking her from seeing what was happening. Matt set a hand beneath her head to bolster it.

The doctor lifted the baby up above the level of the curtain. "Here she is," she announced.

Briar stared, not even daring to breathe. The sight of her daughter was so surreal. Red and wrinkly and so heartbreakingly tiny. So fragile. "Is she breathing?" she demanded.

"Yes, she is," the doctor said, and lowered the baby back behind the curtain. "She's a beauty."

The NICU team took over. Briar dropped her head back to the table and squeezed her eyes shut. Relief and gratitude flooded her. Tears trickled down her temples. She was a mom. She had a daughter. A daughter she couldn't hold right now because the baby was too fragile.

Matt pressed his cheek to hers. "She's beautiful," he said in a choked voice.

Briar nodded and clung to his hands, clamped her lips together and tried to stop crying. At the sound of something being wheeled across the floor, she opened her eyes. The team was pushing an incubator past her. Briar caught one last look at her tiny daughter lying naked on the blanket inside, and then they rushed her out of the room.

A fierce wave of protectiveness rose up, tinged with the sharp edge of panic. If she had been physically able to jump up and run after the baby, she would have.

She reached up and pushed at Matt's shoulder. "Go with her," she begged, unable to stay calm. "You need to go with her."

He wiped the tears from her face. "I don't want to leave you."

"*No.* I'm fine. *Go* with her." She was trapped on the table, frantic with the need to be with her baby. She at least wanted Matt there with her, to make sure everything's okay.

He hesitated, then pressed a kiss to her forehead and got up. "All right. I'll go check on her and see you when you're out of recovery. Don't worry, honey, she's safe and in good hands." He kissed her again. "Love you."

"Love you too," she said, and he left.

The doctor was saying something to her now, something about what she was doing to close the incisions but Briar was past hearing or caring as she wiped at the tears of relief and exhaustion. She didn't care about anything at the moment except her helpless baby daughter who had just been taken away from her.

****

Hard to believe this was real.

Matt stood in front of the large viewing window outside the NICU, still dressed in his scrubs while the team of nurses busily tended to his daughter over in the far back corner. He was still reeling from the events of the past twenty-four hours. He was a *father* now.

His chest tightened as he watched the nurses work on the baby. He and Briar hadn't even picked out names yet, because they'd thought they had lots more time to do it. They had planned to talk about it this weekend during their getaway.

Whatever they decided on, it needed to be special. Maybe something to honor Briar's Palestinian or Venezuelan heritage. Something from the life she'd had with her parents before the accident, before becoming a Valkyrie had changed everything. Though he was grateful for the hardships she'd endured too. Without them, he and Briar would never have met.

A nurse checking on a baby closer to the window noticed him standing here. She popped around the doorway to smile at him. "Are you baby DeLuca's daddy?"

The words hit him unexpectedly hard, like a punch to the ribs. Oh, shit, he was gonna choke up. "Yes."

"Come on in. They've got her all sorted out now, so you can say hi. Just be sure you scrub your hands again as soon as you enter."

His heart thumped in his ears as he walked into the nursery, washed his hands again and headed for the far corner. Another nurse saw him coming, smiled and moved aside a little. "She's doing great. Breathing on her own and her initial vitals look good."

Matt stepped closer, and the sight of his daughter lying there almost snapped the last thread of control he had over his emotions. "She's so tiny," he said, his voice rough.

"Four pounds, nine ounces. That's a good size for a thirty-three weeker."

Barely over four-and-a-half-pounds. Jesus. Her little diaper came up almost to her chest and they'd put what he surmised must be a feed tube into her nose.

He moved closer to the incubator, mesmerized, dying

to touch her. He glanced at the nurse. "Can I...?"

"Of course. You can't hold her just yet, but you can touch her. Go ahead and get acquainted."

Matt drank in every tiny detail of his daughter as he reached in to touch her. The thick cap of dark brown hair on her head, the tiny dark eyebrows and lashes.

His hand looked huge next to her, big enough to cradle her entire body in his palm. She had no fat or muscle on her. He was afraid of hurting her, she was so small and delicate-looking.

Moving cautiously, he reached out his forefinger and gently stroked the thick, fluffy hair on her head. So damn soft, like a baby duckling's down. "How is she?"

"She's doing beautifully. Her suck/swallow reflex isn't well developed yet, but that's normal for this stage. She'll come along fast, you'll see. She's strong."

"She's a warrior, just like her mama." A teensy little Valkyrie, half him, half Briar. God, it was so incredible.

Feeling braver, he reached down to touch one tiny, perfectly-formed hand. She twitched, raised her thin arm and curled those impossibly small fingers around his. Reaching for him. Holding tight, the solid grip surprising him.

A painful squeezing sensation in the middle of his chest stole his breath, his heart swelling so full he didn't even know what to do with it.

"Hello, sweetheart," he said softly, his voice unsteady. "Happy birthday."

The baby's eyes opened a fraction, the gaze hazy and unfocused. But for that split second he was sure she looked at him, and he felt the instant connection between them forge like steel inside him. Unbreakable.

A tissue appeared before his face.

He glanced over at the nurse beside him, not realizing until that moment that he was crying. He wasn't even embarrassed, too overwhelmed to feel anything else. God, he'd never imagined it would feel like this. That he could be this in love this soon.

"Thanks," he murmured and quickly wiped at his eyes, completely overcome.

She grinned. "You're welcome. Moments like this are my favorite part of the job. They more than make the long shifts worthwhile."

Matt went back to studying his daughter, talked to her some more. God, he wished he could hold her. Cuddle her right to his chest so she could feel his heartbeat. She recognized his voice, right? He'd read that somewhere. "You're so beautiful. Your mom and I love you so much already. You've had kind of a rough start, but everything's gonna be okay now." He stroked the back of that little hand with his thumb, drank in every last detail of her, unable to look away.

"I need to check her vitals again," a nurse said gently behind him.

Matt moved aside but didn't pull away, his daughter still clinging to his finger. It slayed him.

Reaching beneath his scrubs into his back jeans pocket, he pulled out his phone to take some pictures. He zoomed in on that tiny hand wrapped around his finger and hit the button, convinced it was the most beautiful and amazing picture anyone had ever taken.

"Here, let me get some of the both of you together," another nurse said.

"Great, thanks." Matt handed her the phone and posed, didn't have to put any effort into the smile that was damn near splitting his face it was so wide. Briar wouldn't be able to come up here for a few hours yet, but he could take this to her along with some video at least. He was so fucking proud of her. She was a fighter, his wife, and the mother of his child. Today she'd given him the most amazing gift in the world.

The nurse gave him back the phone and he sat next to

the incubator for another ten minutes before reluctantly pulling free of his daughter's grip. It tugged at something inside him to leave her, but he needed to see Briar, reassure her everything was fine and make sure she was okay.

"I have to go see your mom now," he told the baby. "She'll be anxious to see these pictures and hear what's going on. But I'll see you soon." He stroked her unbelievably soft cheek with his fingertip. "Love you," he whispered.

"Don't worry, we'll take good care of her," one of the nurses said. "And when your wife comes up from recovery they'll bring her in to see baby."

Matt nodded. "She'd like that."

On the way down to see Briar, a million thoughts and feelings raced through his mind. He was so unbelievably grateful he'd been here for this, but his job had almost prevented it. *This* was what was important. Not his career. Not his team. Not whatever crisis he needed to respond to.

Briar was throwing up into a tray when he entered the recovery room.

Shit. Matt rushed over to wrap an arm under her shoulders to hold her up while the nurse assisted. He laid her back down, took the cloth the nurse handed him and wiped at Briar's damp face.

"This been going on long?" he asked her, smoothing her sweaty hair back from her forehead.

"Long enough," she groaned, and reached for his hand. "How is she?"

He couldn't help but grin. He was so damn proud, totally in love. "She's perfect." The most perfect baby ever born, as far as he was concerned. "She's breathing well, she's warm, and everything's working as it should. They've got a feed tube in her. She held my finger, look." He pulled out his phone and showed her all the pictures.

Briar stared at them all, her eyes suspiciously moist. "I want to see her."

"You will, as soon as they take you upstairs," he promised. God, he wanted to hold Briar, but she was sick and he didn't want to hurt her. "I know we didn't get the chance to talk about this much, but what do you want to name her?"

"I thought she was a boy, so I only picked boys' names. Did you have any girls' names picked out?"

"A few, but I changed my mind once I saw her." He laced their fingers together. "What about something with Rose in it?" Her parents had named her *Wardah*, Arabic for rose. Her Valkyrie handlers had changed it to Briar.

Something soft and vulnerable flashed in her eyes as she gazed up at him. "Oh. I like that."

He did too. And after all Briar had been through, she deserved to have something to honor her past. "Rosalie? Roseanne. Rosemary." No. "Roselynn?"

Her expression brightened. "Roselynn Patricia. After me and your mom."

It touched him that she would suggest it and include his mom that way.

She reached for his phone again, scrolled through the pictures and stopped on the best shot of their daughter's face. "Yeah, Roselynn. But Rosie for short. She looks like a Rosie."

"Rosie," he said, testing the sound of the name. Yeah, it suited her. "Perfect."

Briar smiled at him. "Rosie DeLuca." Then the smile faded and she expelled a hard sigh. "I need to see her."

Matt leaned over to kiss her forehead, squeezed her hand tight. "Soon. I know it's hard. You've both been through a lot, but the tough part's all over and I'm here now to look after both my girls."

He would *always* be here for them.

Chapter Nine

L ying in bed at home nine days later, Briar could hear Matt talking on the phone to his mom in the en suite bathroom. He'd been off work since Rosie's birth and today was his first day back.

These past ten days had been nothing but a blur. Briar had spent the first three in the hospital recovering while Rosie stayed in the NICU for another week. Trinity and the team's significant others had all been amazing, dropping off groceries and meals for them. Briar was sure Taya was behind it. The woman was an organizational wizard.

She and Matt had gone back multiple times a day to hold and feed her, and because Rosie was able to suck and swallow on her own and had been gaining weight, she had finally been able to come home last night. Briar had to feed her every two to three hours, which wasn't a big deal during the day. But overnight was gonna be tough for the next few months.

"We can't wait for you to meet her," Matt was saying. "Maybe I'll bring her with me when I pick you up at the airport, give Briar a few hours to herself."

She smothered a groan. Her mother-in-law and Matt's sister were flying in from San Diego on Thursday night to stay with them a couple days. They were nice people and Briar liked them well enough, but she dreaded having them stay until after the baby shower Taya and Trinity were holding for her this coming weekend.

She didn't feel like having company stay with them yet but he wanted to have them at the house so they could spend as much time with Rosie as possible and she didn't want to cause a fight, so she'd left it alone. He was close with both sides of his family and barely ever got to see them. It wasn't fair of her to tell him they couldn't stay here just because she was uncomfortable having them underfoot because she was ridiculously private and trying to adjust to the whole motherhood thing. And it was only for a few days. She could suck it up for that long.

"Briar? She's doing amazing. Healing up fast and handling everything like a champ."

The pride in Matt's voice set off a twinge of guilt deep inside. Yeah, like a champ. If he only knew how worn down she felt already. Her incisions were healing nicely and she hardly had any pain except for her breasts when they became engorged or whenever Rosie latched on. Taya had been right about that.

"Love you too. Bye." Matt ended the call and came back into the bedroom, walked around to her side of the bed and reached down to stroke a hand over her hair. "I gotta go. You need anything before I leave?"

About twelve hours of uninterrupted sleep would be good, but that wasn't happening. "No." She couldn't even muster the will to inject some life into the answer.

"Okay. See you tonight." He bent and kissed her before leaving.

The moment she heard his truck pull out of the driveway, a heaviness settled inside her chest. He wouldn't be back until at least seven tonight, maybe later.

That meant she had a minimum of twelve hours to get through on her own, even though she'd been the one to argue that she was fine by herself now and encouraged him to go into work. At the moment, the prospect of being without him all day seemed like an eternity.

She fell back asleep until Rosie's cry woke her from a deep dream. She peeled her eyes open and got up, walked on auto-pilot down the hall to the nursery.

Briar picked her up, checked her diaper that was still dry, and sat in the chair to nurse her. They'd switched from cannula feeding to nursing last week, and they were both still getting the hang of it. The latching bit was tricky. And painful.

Briar winced as the baby tried to latch on, a feeling like hot, sharp prickles shooting through her breasts as the milk let down. Breastfeeding was way harder than she had imagined, and way more uncomfortable as well. She pumped to alleviate the pressure when she got too engorged but it still hurt like hell and it happened often because Rosie couldn't yet drain one side per feeding.

All in all, motherhood was harder than she had expected. She was constantly exhausted, sore all over. Maybe it was because of all the complications and running back and forth to the NICU. She kept hoping everything would smooth out now that they were home.

Rosie was still slightly jaundiced, even after treatment in the hospital. Frequent nursing would help, but she was so small her esophageal sphincter hadn't yet fully developed. Briar could only feed her a little bit at a time, and the milk quite often came right back up a few minutes later, projectile-style, leaving Rosie hungry and Briar frustrated.

Basically, she felt like she didn't know what the hell she was doing. Worse, she didn't feel this magical bond everyone always talked about between mother and child. She loved Rosie, was doing her best to look after her baby.

But it all felt so strange, the opposite of natural. Probably being separated for the first ten days hadn't helped. Briar hoped it happened soon.

Trinity had offered to come stay with her after Rosie had finally come home, but Briar didn't want to put her friend out and didn't want to admit she needed help. She had this. She was strong and resourceful. Tough. A freaking *Valkyrie*. Everyone else seemed to manage with being able to look after a newborn, so she could too.

Part way through the feeding, Rosie choked and turned her head away, spraying milk everywhere.

"Shit," Briar whispered, grabbing for a cloth. She worried that was going to be Rosie's first word.

She couldn't stop the flow of milk. Her body desperately wanted to relieve the pressure in her breasts. Pumping only helped so much, but the lactation specialists had warned her and Matt not to feed Rosie by bottle too often, or she wouldn't learn to latch properly.

It took another half-hour to get enough milk into Rosie to make her feel full. Briar tucked the baby to her chest and burped her gently, then sat and rocked her for a while to keep her upright and help the milk settle. The feel of that tiny, warm little body curled so trustingly against her made her heart squeeze, gave her hope that their mysterious bond was happening.

When Rosie was fast asleep, Briar picked her up and put her back in her crib, desperate to go back to bed for another hour. She was just easing the nursery door shut when she heard the telltale wet splash behind her. Closing her eyes for a moment, she took a deep breath and fought back her frustration.

When she turned around, she spotted the milk stain arcing across the wall beside the crib.

Shit. Milk wasted. Mess to clean up. More laundry to do. And back to square one for another attempt at feeding.

By the time it was all done another forty minutes had

passed. Briar finally left her daughter asleep in the crib and carried the dirty linens and sleeper to the laundry room to start another load.

A pile of neatly folded clothes and receiving blankets lay atop the drier where Matt had placed them last night. He helped out with what he could when he was home. Laundry, grocery runs, bringing home takeout, bathing or changing Rosie. He'd even taken over a feeding with a bottle last night because he'd insisted, but some stubborn part of her made her want to prove she could do it all.

As she walked back into their bedroom, her body heavy and aching with exhaustion, her cell rang. She glanced at the screen to see if it was important, ready to ignore it if it wasn't.

Taya. Probably calling about the shower this weekend. At the moment, not as important as getting more sleep.

Briar set the phone down on the bedside table and sank onto the mattress. She didn't want a baby shower. She didn't want houseguests. She wanted peace and quiet and sleep, just her, Matt and Rosie.

When she lay down and tugged the covers over her, the phone rang again. This time it was Trinity. Briar stared at it a moment, made up her mind to tell her friend how she felt about the shower. So she answered.

"Hey, how are you feeling today?" Trinity asked brightly.

"I don't think I've ever been this tired before. Not even during training."

Trinity chuckled. "Rosie running you ragged already?"

"We're still trying to figure out a routine." She drew in a breath. "Look, I know it's late to do this, and I really appreciate all the trouble you've gone to in organizing everything, but I think we should cancel the shower."

"What? Why?"

Because I'm fucking wrecked and I don't feel like

having to socialize with a bunch of people. "Matt's mom and sister are coming in the night before. I'm gonna be busy. It's too much."

"I've already talked to Matt's mom. She and Matt's sister are going to set everything up, take care of the cleaning, cooking and laundry so you can focus on Rosie. You don't have to do anything except eat and open the gifts."

Hell. Briar bit back a sigh. What was wrong with her? The women coming over were her friends and extended family. Most other women would be ecstatic about their friends throwing them a shower.

"I know parties aren't your thing, but you literally don't have to do anything but show up," Trinity went on. "Rosie's the main attraction, not you. If you're not feeling up to it when we get there, you can always stay upstairs to sleep for a while and let us look after the baby. Then you can come down when you're ready and in more of a party mood. And it's only for a couple hours. We'll be out of your hair by dinnertime, and we'll clean everything up so you don't have to do a thing. There'll be lots of leftovers, too."

Well, leftovers were good. And she didn't want to seem like an ungrateful bitch. She was tired and cranky as hell, but that didn't excuse her from being rude to anyone else, let alone the people who loved her. "Okay, you're right. Thanks."

"It'll be great, you'll see," Trinity said excitedly. "Everyone can't wait to see you and Rosie."

****

Show time.

Squaring her shoulders, Briar lifted her chin and checked her reflection in the bathroom mirror. The shower was about to start.

She had covered the dark circles under her eyes with concealer, something she'd never bought in her entire life until this morning, but it was necessary to make her look human. Last night had been tough even with Matt helping and she hadn't caught up on enough sleep between Rosie's feedings this morning.

At the moment the guys were all at Bauer and Zoe's place to hang out for the afternoon. She was glad that Matt was getting the downtime. In between returning to work and helping out overnight with Rosie, he had to be tired too. His mom and sister were downstairs with the baby right now, watching her while Briar got ready. They were great with her, and it was nice to have a little time to herself.

Her mother-in-law gave Briar a smile when she walked into the kitchen. Pat had Rosie expertly cuddled into one shoulder while she stirred a pot of something on the stove. "This little one's getting hungry again, I think," she said, turning to Briar.

"I'm sure she is." Briar took her daughter, the way Rosie melted into her hold making her smile.

She went into the living room and sat on the sofa to nurse her while Matt's sister Karen bustled around the room setting up the table and putting up decorations. Everything was pink. Pink balloons. Pink streamers. Pink flowers and tablecloth.

"You guys really didn't have to go to so much trouble," Briar said as she arranged a blanket over her chest and maneuvered Rosie into place to nurse. She bit down on the inside of her cheek and hid a wince when those hard little gums clamped onto her sore nipple.

"It's no trouble. Besides, it's Rosie's first party," Karen said, beaming.

Trinity and Taya arrived a few minutes later. Briar stayed where she was, angling her face up to accept the cheek kisses from her friends.

"How's our little piglet of honor doing today?" Taya asked, shifting Hudson on her hip. He was crawling now. Wouldn't be long until he was walking.

"She's trying her best to suck me dry but she just can't take a full feeding yet." Briar felt bad for her. Poor little thing was always hungry.

"Well, top her up then. She'll be ready to be passed around when everyone else gets here." She focused on Briar. "How are you feeling today? Nursing getting any easier?"

"Pretty good, actually. And sort of." Matt had taken a feeding at two this morning, allowing her to get another bit of sleep. She didn't feel quite like a zombie at the moment.

"I'm glad. Can I get you anything?"

"No, I'm good."

"Okay, I'm just going to set up the playpen and put Hudson in it so he'll stay out of trouble."

As soon as Briar finished feeding and burping Rosie, she handed the baby to Trinity. It was bittersweet to watch her friend hold Rosie. Trinity's whole face lit up, her enjoyment obvious. Briar hoped she would consider adopting at some point.

The rest of the guests arrived in two groups. Briar forced herself into social mode and introduced everyone to Karen and Pat, then parked her butt on the "throne" they'd made for her. It actually helped to have her friends around. She'd been dreading this, but now that they were all here she felt so much less overwhelmed and isolated.

For some reason the days seemed to be better for her than the nights. By mid-morning she had usually managed to sneak in another hour or two of sleep in between feedings. After showering, she felt almost like herself.

The nights were a different story. She had already come to dread them. Each evening around dinnertime, some sort of switch inside her flipped. A kind of panic crept in at the thought of facing another long, sleepless night looking after Rosie alone.

She didn't get it. With her training and background, considering the kind of punishment and deprivation she'd been trained to withstand, it made no sense that she would feel that way. And she definitely didn't want Matt to know she was struggling.

"All right, now that we're all stuffing our faces," Zoe said, pushing to her feet as Libby and Hudson played with toys in the playpen nearby, "it's time to start the games."

Briar groaned. Several of the women laughed, but Zoe shot her a narrow-eyed look. "Yeah, I know you think that's right up there with torture. But you haven't played my games." She waggled her dark eyebrows.

"So what've you got for us?" Carm demanded.

"A little something I like to call porn versus labor."

Huh? Briar frowned in confusion as Zoe pulled out a folder and passed it to Carm. "Take one and a pen, and pass it around."

Marisol took them and gave it to Briar. Briar pulled out a sheet of paper with a dozen different photos on it, each of them a close up of a woman's face either in the throes of…well, it could be orgasm or agony, it was impossible to tell which.

"You have to guess whether each picture is from porn or labor," Zoe explained. "Person with the most right answers wins."

Man, romantic horror authors had sick minds. Briar eyed her sheet. "Tell me you didn't find these while doing research for your new book."

"I didn't," Zoe said. "But that would have been *amazing*."

"What do we win?" Taya asked, already writing down her answers. Keener.

"Prizes."

"Yeah, but what kind of prizes."

"*Awesome* ones," Zoe said confidently.

Briar studied the images. Jeez, she had no freaking clue what was what. There was only one that seemed to obviously be labor. A few minutes later they traded papers and marked them while Zoe gave the answers.

"Okay, how many did you guys get?" Zoe asked.

"I got eight," Karen said.

"Ten," Carmella answered.

Zoe looked at Briar. "How many did you get?"

"Two."

Those golden eyes widened. "Two? What? Gimme that." She snatched Briar's paper to read it. "How could you only get two?"

She glowered. "They all look like they're enjoying themselves to me."

Zoe laughed, a low, throaty sound. "Really? What the hell has Matt been doing to you all this time?"

She flushed, even though Zoe was just teasing. "Well, I didn't go through labor, so…"

"All right. Moving on," Zoe said, handing out prizes to the winner. "You get the pity prize," told Briar.

Briar opened the bag. Eyes wide, she looked up at Zoe. "Really?" A sex toy? And a dubious-looking one at that.

Zoe smirked. "Glows in the dark."

Of course it did.

"You won't be able to use it for a while yet, but when you do, you'll thank me. *Trust* me."

Okaaay then. She was sure Matt would get a giant kick out of it.

The afternoon passed by fairly quickly after that. Food, drinks and presents. Rosie even got a cute little camo dress from Trinity and pajamas that said *My Mom's A Badass* across the chest from Summer. Briar kept an eagle eye on her daughter as the baby was passed around the room. She trusted all the women in the room, but this was her baby and she was going to make sure Rosie was being held properly.

"You look fantastic, by the way," Rachel said to her, looking her up and down. "Can't even tell you had a baby a couple weeks ago."

"Thanks." Everyone kept saying that. That she looked great, seemed to be handling everything with ease, even with Rosie's challenges as a preemie.

Looks could be deceiving, however. At times she had been more miserable since Rosie's birth than she ever had, except for when her parents died and she was first taken into the Valkyrie Program. It was a constant grind to hide that from the rest of the world, including Matt, but there was no way she was going to show the truth.

At four the guests began leaving. By five, it was only her in-laws, Taya and Trinity left. They refused to let Briar clean up, ordering her to sit on her throne while they cleaned up and organized all the presents.

"I put everything away in her room," Trinity said as she emerged from the bottom of the staircase, "but you can reorganize it later."

"Thanks." She carefully removed her sleeping daughter from her breast, covered back up, and put Rosie to her shoulder to burp.

Trinity held out her hands. "May I?"

"Of course." She handed Trinity the blanket to drape over her shoulder.

Trinity took Rosie and carefully tucked her close. She patted the baby's back gently. "God, she even smells good," she murmured.

"I know, right?"

"Until they start eating solids," Taya called from the kitchen. "Then not so much."

Trinity grinned at Briar. "Ah, the things you get to look forward to, huh?"

"Yeah, I can't wait."

Rosie belched, and the telltale splash followed a

second later, all over Trinity.

Briar sighed. "Sorry about that. You've been christened. Welcome to the church of projectile vomiting."

"It's okay." Trinity held Rosie away from her a little. "Got me, you little stinker. But you're adorable, so I forgive you." She wiped at the mess on her shirt the blanket hadn't protected her from with a cloth and handed Rosie back to Briar. "Here ya go, mama. Fill her back up and I'll talk to you tomorrow." She dropped a kiss on Briar's cheek.

"Thanks for everything," Briar said.

"You bet. See you."

Watching Trinity leave, Briar had to fight the urge to call her back. Ask her to stay. She could feel herself starting to slide emotionally, the anxiety building as the coming night loomed before her, dark and endless.

Chapter Ten

———————

Since it was the weekend, traffic was light on the way home. Matt couldn't wait to get into the house as he pulled into their driveway. Hanging with the guys for the day, watching his Chargers defeat their opponent while eating pizza and drinking beer had been a nice break. But he'd missed his girls and was dying to see them.

His mom and sister were in the final phase of cleaning up the kitchen when he walked in through the mudroom. He hugged them both, asked a couple questions to be polite and not make it seem like he didn't care about them even though what he really wanted was to go straight up to see Briar and Rosie.

Finally his mom laughed at him. "You don't care about talking to us, you just want to see your baby. Go." She shooed him, popped him on the back with the dishtowel as he walked away.

He jogged upstairs to find Briar. She was in the nursery, feeding Rosie in the comfy chair, and looked up with a greeting smile when he pushed the door open. The sight of her and Rosie together still hit him hard, filled his heart full to bursting with love and pride. "Hey, how are the two most important women in my life doing?"

"We survived."

He chuckled at her dry response and crossed to them. "Glad to hear it, but I had complete faith in you." He bent to kiss her softly, ran a hand over her hair as he pulled the edge of the nursing blanket aside to peer at their daughter. Rosie was curled up in Briar's arms, her little mouth barely moving at Briar's breast. "She all done?"

"For now. She got Trinity good just before she left, so I had to feed her again. I'm hoping most of it will stay down this time."

"I'll take her," he said, easing her from Briar's hold. Rosie released the nipple with a pop, stretched her thin arms over her head, her little face scrunching, then curled up into the fetal position once more and drifted off.

God, she was the most freaking adorable thing he'd ever seen, her tiny body slightly larger now than when she'd been born. She'd gained almost two pounds since coming home.

He tossed a burp cloth over his shoulder and tucked her against it, the feel of her cuddled against him filling him with a simultaneous protectiveness and tenderness on a level he'd never imagined possible before she came along. The thick mop of dark hair on her head was so damn soft. He nuzzled it, cradled her to him as he wrapped a light blanket around her.

Briar stood with a sigh and stretched, putting her hands to her lower back. Matt glanced at her. She was holding up amazingly well considering she'd had major surgery not quite two weeks ago, and had never complained about pain or anything even though she insisted on doing almost everything herself. Not that he was surprised. "You tired?"

She shrugged. "A little."

That she would admit even that much told him she was actually exhausted. And the shower today would have worn her out more than usual. Having his mom and sister here right now made her feel a little awkward as well, but they were leaving tomorrow. He'd made sure the visit was only three days, max. "Why don't you go lie down for a while? I'll take the princess downstairs so it'll be nice and quiet. Do you have a bottle ready?"

"There's a whole stockpile in the fridge." She followed him to the doorway, hesitated at the start of the hallway. "You sure?"

The truth was, he wanted to be more involved, feel like he was pulling his weight with all the things that came along with taking care of a baby. Briar didn't let him do much to help her and it frustrated him sometimes. "Yeah, of course. Go to bed." Brushing a quick kiss across her mouth, he went downstairs. In the living room he lowered himself to the couch, stretched out his legs as he laid Rosie more comfortably across his chest.

"Aww," his mom said, and rushed in from the kitchen with Karen to take another million pictures and some video on her phone. "I just can't get over seeing you with her. I always knew you'd be a good dad, but this is so…" She sniffed, bit her lip.

Matt chuckled. "Yeah, she's got me wrapped nice and tight around her little finger already." So far, fatherhood had surpassed his highest expectations. He'd never felt so fulfilled or content. So complete.

Rosie was the first thing he thought about when he opened his eyes, and the last one he thought about before closing them. He couldn't wait to get home from work just to hold her. It was still incredible to him. After Lisa died, he'd thought he would never have the chance to be a father. Now that he was, he couldn't imagine not having Rosie in his life.

"Where's Briar?" Karen asked.

"I told her to get some sleep. She doesn't get much overnight, especially if Rosie doesn't keep her milk down. I'm taking the next feeding." They'd arranged it so he would take at least one each night to let Briar sleep a bit more, and she insisted on doing the rest during the week because he had to get up early for work. He'd gone into the office these past few days to get some things finished up while his mom and sister were here to lend a hand.

Nothing had come up yet that required him to go out of town since the birth, though it was only a matter of time before it did. Both teams had training ops next month with SOF units, and then there were whatever situations they were called in for.

"Well Karen and I can each take a turn feeding Rosie a bottle overnight," his mom said.

"Thanks, but Briar has to get up to pump anyway." She was also a really private and independent person, so no matter how good his mom and sister's intentions were, Briar would prefer to do it all herself. She was adorably protective of Rosie, watching like a hawk anytime someone other than him was holding their daughter.

"She seems to be doing well with everything. It must have been a huge adjustment to her at first, especially after the emergency C-section and all the running back and forth to the NICU until Rosie came home," his mom said.

Matt nodded. "Briar's amazing. She can handle anything." He'd never been prouder of his wife than these weeks since Rosie was born. Her strength through everything made him feel weak by comparison. He just wanted to be more involved with Rosie. "I do what I can to give her a break when I'm home, but she's doing the lion's share of it."

"I hope I can come out and spend more time with you guys now, or that you'll fly back to California to visit more often. I hate living so far away from my only grandchild."

He hid a smile. His mom—and Karen for that matter—would love nothing more than to be Briar's bestie. She was having a hard time accepting that Briar hadn't yet warmed up to her the way she wanted. She didn't know about Briar's background, or understand why she was so cautious and guarded around people she didn't know. Matt had only told his mother that Briar was former military and left it at that, because there were a lot of things in Briar's past that she didn't want people to know about.

Briar would warm up to her though eventually, given enough time. His mom was a fantastic lady. He'd told her to be patient with Briar. They just needed to let the relationship develop naturally, spend more time together over the coming months and not force it.

"We'd like that too," he said, sharing a knowing smile with his sister.

His mom beamed at him. "Well. If you get tired of holding her, let me know. I'm ready for another turn."

"Yeah, and me too," Karen said. "I only got to hold her for all of five minutes this afternoon with all the other women hogging her."

"Will do," Matt said, and settled back against the cushions to visit with his family. But he was never going to get tired of holding Rosie. Ever.

****

Briar opened her eyes in the darkness when the baby's cries woke her, her heart kicking into overdrive. When she realized it was real and not a dream, she stifled a whimper of exhaustion.

No, no, she begged Rosie silently. *Go back to sleep. Please go back to sleep.* It was too soon for another feeding. Briar had only fallen asleep a few minutes ago, she was sure of it.

The cries continued.

Matt was somehow still asleep beside her and she didn't want to wake him because he had to be up early for work. His mother and sister were in the downstairs guestroom and she didn't want to wake them either.

You wanted this. This is part of being a mom. Get up.

Dragging herself upright, she threw her legs over the side of the bed, pushed to her feet. She felt drunk, weaving on her feet a little as she grabbed her robe from the end of the bed and headed for the door, her eyes still half-closed.

Unable to shake the lingering fog in her brain, she pushed aside the fatigue and stumbled down the hall toward the nursery. Rosie's cries were now outraged wails of hunger. Briar turned toward the door, slammed into the corner wall and bounced off it on her way by. She cursed, shook her head to clear it as she entered the room.

Shutting the door behind her to muffle Rosie's cries throughout the rest of the house, Briar didn't bother flipping on the lamp before picking her daughter up out of the crib and moved to the nursing chair. Rosie stopped crying immediately and began fussing instead, turning her face toward Briar's chest, rooting impatiently for a breast.

Briar sat in the chair in the dark, pulled her robe and nightgown open to expose her nursing bra, and undid one side. Rosie practically attacked the nipple, and the feel of those gums clamping tight around it made Briar cringe.

She bit her lip, toes curling as the pain rushed through her, the hot needling sensation coming next as the milk began to flow. Rosie swallowed twice then choked, turning her head away.

"No," Briar whispered, holding the cloth up to stop the milk from spraying everywhere. "Come *on*." She put Rosie back in place, and the baby latched on again, triggering more pain. God, when was this going to get easier? Nursing felt anything but natural to her. She actually dreaded it, and that made her feel like a bad mom.

A few minutes later Rosie began to slow her suckling. "Nuh-uh, you're going to finish all of it, because I need more than thirty minutes' sleep at a time," Briar told her, tapping her little cheek to wake her. Rosie began to suckle faster again, but soon slowed once more.

Briar sighed. Trying to force Rosie to stay awake and eat more was pointless.

She gave up, removed the nearly asleep baby from her breast and lifted Rosie to burp her. She got a tiny one for her efforts, sat and rocked Rosie for another minute. When all seemed calm, she put her back in the crib and crept to the door.

Reaching for the handle, a soft choking sound stopped her. Briar froze. It came again. Whirling, she hit the light. Rosie's little face was red and no sound was coming out.

She didn't even remember moving to the crib, just grabbed the baby and banged a firm hand on her back.

A giant wet splash all over the front of her was her reward.

Briar closed her eyes, the smell of regurgitated milk in her nostrils as her daughter began to fuss again from hunger.

Just like that, something inside her broke.

She dropped back into the chair, the wall she'd hidden everything behind these past two weeks suddenly collapsing to dust. And just like that, she crumbled.

The tears she'd held in for so long poured from her without her permission, hard, tight sobs wrenching from her chest. They burned her throat, hurt her ribs. Her heart.

This was horrible. She was overwhelmed. Exhausted wasn't even strong enough a word for how tired she was. It felt like she was trapped in a dark tunnel and she couldn't see any light at the end.

What the hell had she done? She'd wanted a child and now she was stuck in this constant hell of sleep deprivation, doubt and pain. She felt so alone. Was too ashamed to tell anyone what was going on.

She couldn't tell Matt how she really felt. What kind of mother was she to be feeling like this? What would he think of her if he knew? She had never seen Matt so happy, utterly in love with being a dad, while she was falling to pieces. It made her feel even worse.

There was no way to ignore the truth any longer. Her deepest fear about becoming a mother had been realized.

Something was wrong with her, missing inside her. She wasn't equipped for this. And now their daughter was saddled with a dysfunctional mother for the rest of her life.

Briar's hand shook as she fumbled with the other side of her bra, managed to get it undone but couldn't stop crying as she helped Rosie latch on. She clamped her lips together, choked back the sobs as they ripped through her, afraid Matt would hear her. She couldn't bear for him to see her like this. Couldn't bear for him to learn the truth.

That his fierce Valkyrie was a fraud, and falling apart under the strain of being a mother.

Chapter Eleven

T he house was dead quiet when Matt walked into the kitchen after work the following Thursday night. His mom and sister had flown out on Monday, so Briar had been alone all day without any help for the week—at her insistence. She had to be tired and he loved spelling her off when he got home because it was pretty much the only time he got to hold and take care of Rosie.

He set the Indian takeout on the counter and headed for the stairs, excited to see her and Briar. The baby had grown so much already, he hated being away from her so long every day and didn't want to miss a single milestone.

He stopped in surprise at the bottom of the stairs when he spotted Briar on the couch with the baby. Her eyes were open, her head bent. She didn't look up at him, didn't acknowledge his presence even though he knew she must have heard him come in.

A subtle tension took hold in his stomach, instinct warning him that something wasn't right.

"Hey," he said softly, walking toward her. She wasn't

nursing Rosie. Just holding her as the baby slept.

"Hi," she said, finally looking up at him. Dark smudges lay beneath her eyes and he thought he saw shadows in them as well, but maybe they seemed so dark because the only light in the room was a lamp on in the corner.

Concerned, Matt sat down next to her. "You okay?"

She nodded. "How was your day?"

"Good." She wasn't okay. "Rough day?"

A tight shrug. "Not really."

"How's Rosie?"

"Fine. She managed to hold down everything for all the feedings except one time today."

"That's great." Briar didn't seem too excited about it, however. He studied her, unsure what was wrong, and she was in no hurry to tell him. "I brought dinner from your favorite Indian place. You hungry?"

"I could eat."

"I'll get you a plate." He went to the kitchen and put a plate together for the both of them, glancing up at her every so often. She reached for the remote and switched the TV on, settled on a comedy sitcom she liked, but he got the feeling it was more to fill the silence and discourage him from trying to talk to her more than anything else.

He carried the plates in and waited until she set Rosie in the bassinet before giving her one. Unsure what he was supposed to do—should he try to get her to talk about whatever was bothering her, or just let it go—he ate with her in silence. She ate everything on her plate, downed the glass of water he brought her, but it was like someone had hit a dimmer switch and doused the light inside her.

He cleaned up the dishes and put the leftovers away, then joined her on the couch again. The instant he sat down, she leaned into him, tucking her hands against his ribs as she laid her head on his shoulder without a word.

Seeking out comfort.

Something twisted in the center of his chest. He lifted his arm, wrapped it around her and pulled her in close. Except for sex—which they hadn't had since the birth and wouldn't for weeks yet—or maybe reaching for his hand or the occasional hug, she didn't often initiate or seek out affection. The way she cuddled into him now told him something was definitely wrong, rousing his protective instincts.

He kissed the top of her head, rubbed his hand over her back, considering his approach carefully. "Tired?"

She nodded.

That and her continued silence were starting to really worry him. She was taking on too much by herself. He would broach the idea of hiring a nanny or housekeeper tomorrow. "Let's stretch out and you can snooze on me," he suggested, shifting away from her for a moment.

She grabbed at his shirt and pressed closer, as if afraid he might leave her. Hiding her face as she clung to him.

His strong, independent wife was fucking *clinging* to him like he was a life vest and she was drowning.

Startled, Matt froze and looked down at her. He couldn't see her face. He raised his free hand to settle a finger beneath her chin so he could tip her face up, felt her shoulders shake. Once. Twice. Small, jerky motions.

Holy shit, was she *crying*?

Alarmed, he pulled back and took her face in his hands. "Hey. What's wrong?"

She pushed his hands aside and burrowed her face into his chest, refusing to look at him as she continued to hold onto his shirt, her upper body jerking. She didn't make a sound as she cried, and it broke his heart.

What the hell? "Honey, hey. No, look at me." He finally eased her away far enough that he could see her face, and the tear tracks on her cheeks. His shirt had wet spots on it. "What's the matter?"

"I don't *know*," she cried, and shoved her face back into his chest.

Dumbfounded, not knowing what the hell was going on or what to do, Matt leaned back and pulled her closer, wrapped both arms around her to hold her tight. He could count on one hand the number of times he'd seen her cry. He'd seen her withstand pain and devastating things that would crush most people, and she'd never come unglued like this.

No joke, seeing her this distraught alarmed him. But that she didn't seem to know what was wrong worried him even more.

Briar continued to cry her silent tears, the occasional hitching gasp escaping despite her best efforts to stifle them. He could feel her fighting to stop, feel her battling for control. He didn't know what the hell to say or what to do except hold her until she was finished.

Finally, the gasps stopped and turned to shuddering sighs. He relaxed his grip, stroked her long, gorgeous hair. It was like she was broken. Why was she so sad? "Okay. Now talk to me," he demanded in as gentle a tone as he could manage considering his concern.

Briar groaned and sat up, impatiently wiping her face with her hands, avoiding his gaze and his words.

No way. He wasn't letting this go. If she was fucking crying, whatever it was, was bad. "Briar. Tell me what's wrong." He'd fix it. Kick someone's ass for her. Slay dragons. Anything to make this better.

She shook her head. "I don't know," she repeated in a lost tone.

"Well something is," he said in exasperation. "Is it... Are you overtired? Or sore? Getting sick?" An infection from the operation, or maybe the start of mastitis. He put a hand to her forehead, frowned. Her cheeks were flushed, but she wasn't warm.

She looked at him, those piercing dark eyes puffy and

swollen, so full of misery and heartache it stunned him. "You really wanna know?" She raised one eyebrow, almost in defiance.

Matt weighed his options, trying to figure out how best to handle this. "Yes. What's going on?"

She inhaled deeply, let it out nice and slow, and her expression hardened. "Fine. I've been sitting here for the past two hours holding our daughter, and thinking the same thing over and over. I can't get it out of my head."

"Thinking what?"

The hard edge to her expression faded, replaced again by a deep sadness that scared him a little. "That we brought this baby into the world, and now because of our selfishness, she'll have to suffer and die one day," she finished, her voice catching on the last few words.

Matt stared at her in disbelief, not knowing how he was supposed to respond to that. "What?" he said finally.

She shrugged, lifted a hand in a helpless gesture. "I know. I know it's stupid, but it's all I can think about." She swallowed, seemed to fight for her composure for a moment before continuing. "I hold her and look down at her sweet, innocent little face, and all I can think about is how much she'll suffer at the end, and it's all our fault."

Holy. Shit.

Matt tried not to gape at her. He really did. But Jesus Christ, that was so out there he didn't know what to think. Other than *clearly* she wasn't doing well. At all.

He glanced at Rosie, sound asleep in her bassinet, and made a snap decision. "Okay. Up you get." He stood, scooped her up in his arms and started for the stairs.

"Where are we going?" she said, pushing at his shoulders.

He ignored her, tightened his grip and kept going. "Upstairs. I'm putting you to bed."

"I don't need to go to bed—"

"Yes, you do. You're totally exhausted and you need

to sleep." He stopped on the bottom stair and searched her eyes. He hated that sad, haunted look in them. "Honey, you're done in. Let me look after Rosie while you get some sleep. You'll feel way better when you wake up." He hoped.

Her shoulders drooped and she put her head on his shoulder, almost in defeat. But she allowed him to take her upstairs where he pulled the covers back, settled her under them and then literally tucked her in. "Just sleep," he whispered, bending to kiss her forehead. "Love you."

"Love you too." She reached for his hand, held tight for a long moment before letting go.

Matt closed the door and headed back downstairs, his thoughts churning. He hadn't noticed anything was wrong until tonight. Had he missed the signs? She hid things so well. But thinking about Rosie suffering and dying one day? That wasn't normal, was it? She wasn't even three weeks old yet.

He stood in the living room, hands on hips, and decided he needed backup on this one. Phoning Briar's doctor seemed premature right now. Calling his mom was out. This was too personal and Briar would freak if he told his mom.

Schroder was a medic, and a new dad. Matt could talk to him, get his opinion without giving too much away. But Taya and Briar were close. If Schroder told Taya, she would be on their doorstep first thing tomorrow morning to talk to Briar about it. Nope.

Blackwell. He and Summer had been through a lot of tough times and emotional upheaval on their journey to finally becoming parents, and they'd finally had Sam last year. Maybe they would have some insight, or at least know something he could do or say to make Briar feel better.

Careful to keep his voice down, he sat on the couch close to the bassinet and called Blackwell. "Hi," Matt said

when the other man answered. "I just got home and..."
Found my tough as nails wife having an emotional breakdown. "Do you have a minute to talk?"

"Sure," Blackwell said, sounding surprised. "What's up?"

He kept his voice down, making sure Briar couldn't hear him from upstairs. "You and Summer went through a lot together before Sam came along."

"Yeah."

"And it was especially tough on Summer, you said."

"Definitely. Why, what's going on?"

He ignored the question for the moment. "When she was really upset, what did you find worked the best to help her?"

"Matt. Answer the damn question so I know what's going on."

He expelled a deep breath. "Briar's not doing so well."

"No?"

"No." He explained what had happened, then waited.

"Whoa," Blackwell said. "That's..."

Dark? Scary? "I know," Matt muttered. "I don't know what the hell to do about it. I just put her to bed, hoping a good night's sleep will help."

"Well I— Hang on," he said, and Matt could hear Summer in the background. "Here, I'm gonna let Summer field this one."

Matt hadn't wanted to involve anyone else, but what the hell, and as a new mom who had been through her share of ups and downs, Summer might have valuable insight. He told her the same thing he'd told her husband. "So I put her to bed. She needed sleep in the worst way."

Summer snorted. "Yeah, I'm gonna give you a pass on that one just because you didn't know any better. But what you should have done? Was just hold her."

"I did. It didn't help."

"And just *keep* holding her until she felt strong enough

to let go," Summer said, then sighed as if in disappointment.

"Has she got...postpartum, do you think?" He didn't know much about it, but that term scared him.

"I don't know if it's that serious, but it sounds to me like she's definitely got the baby blues."

His immediate reaction was to reject the idea, but he reined it in. She was definitely sad and overtired. Had there been signs before now and he just hadn't noticed? "Tonight's the first time I've ever seen her like this. Honest, she's been a total trooper up 'til now."

"Well yeah, but hello, you do know this is Briar we're talking about, right? She doesn't want you or anyone else to know she's struggling so she's been putting on a brave front until now. It sounds like tonight she finally reached her limit, for whatever reason. Google the difference between baby blues and postpartum and do some reading, but I think baby blues usually happens sooner and it's also really common for new moms. Pretty sure postpartum develops later and lasts longer, plus it's more serious."

God, he hoped it was just the baby blues and not the other. "I'll do some research and talk to her doctor in the morning."

"And don't forget, Briar's had an even rougher time through all of this because of the traumatic birth and all the extra care Rosie needs as a preemie."

"Right. I'll read up on all that, take care of Rosie overnight so Briar can sleep. I'll take some time off, maybe hire outside help."

"Good. And while you're doing all that, just be there for her. It's hard for her to ask or admit to any form of weakness, so you're probably going to have to intervene and force her to talk about it. You want me to pop over to see her tomorrow?"

"No, and don't tell her I told you guys. She'd be embarrassed." And he'd be in deep shit.

"All right. But keep your eye on her. If it gets worse or lasts longer than another week or so, I'd think about getting her doctor or maybe a psychologist involved."

"Okay. Thanks, Summer."

"Of course. Call us if you need anything. I'll lie like a rug in front of Briar if you want me to come over, pretend I don't know anything about what's going on."

This was why he loved and felt privileged to be the team's commander. They were a family and always willing to help each other out. "Will do. G'night."

He hung up, blew out a breath and looked over at his sleeping daughter. He hated seeing Briar so upset. He wanted to help her through this, but he couldn't if she wouldn't put aside her stubborn pride and be honest with him.

****

Briar opened her eyes expecting complete darkness, and was surprised that it was already getting light out. Morning? What the hell time was it?

She rolled over, winced as her engorged breasts squashed against the mattress. It was after seven, which meant she'd had more than eight hours of sleep.

In a row. Without being woken up once.

She looked down at herself. Her breasts were full to bursting. She didn't remember feeding Rosie after Matt got home and…

Oh, God. She closed her eyes as last night came flooding back. That horrifyingly embarrassing meltdown.

Her insides tightened with dread at the thought of facing Matt this morning. He must think she had lost her damn mind.

And Rosie. She must be starving.

Briar threw on her robe, quickly brushed her teeth and hair and rushed out into the hall. The nursery door was open, the crib empty. Matt must have her downstairs. Was he still home?

She hurried down the stairs, turned the corner and stopped dead at the sight that greeted her in the living room. Matt was stretched out on his back on the couch, fast asleep, with Rosie curled up on his broad chest, one big hand cradled over her back.

The sight of them turned her heart over.

Instead of waking them she grabbed her phone and came back to take pictures. She was straightening from bending over for a close up when Matt's eyes popped open. He blinked up at her, glanced down at Rosie then back at her.

"Morning," she whispered. "You were down here all night?" There were three empty bottles sitting on the coffee table beside him, so she guessed he had been.

He gingerly sat up, careful not to disturb Rosie. "Yeah. What time is it?"

"Seven. Here, I'll take her up and change her." She lifted Rosie, cuddled her close to kiss the top of her fluffy little head. She felt awful for the way she'd been last night.

"Already did about an hour ago. She should sleep for a while longer yet."

Guilt settled inside her, prickly and sharp. He'd been out here on the couch all night handling everything alone to let her sleep because she'd had some sort of breakdown. "I've either gotta feed her or pump, before I burst." Thankfully Rosie woke up and immediately started rooting. Briar latched her onto one side, sighed in relief as Rosie began to suckle and ease the pressure in her swollen breast.

"How are you feeling?" Matt asked, and at any other time she would have rolled her eyes at his cautious approach. As if he was afraid of setting her off if he said the wrong thing.

Now she couldn't meet his eyes as she answered. "Much better. Thanks."

"Of course." When she started to turn away, he caught her arm, stopping her. "Can we talk about last night?"

She cringed inside. She'd been dreading this, having to confront her behavior in the harsh light of day. But even though she felt fantastic at the moment, she couldn't deny she wasn't always handling things well.

"Come on," he coaxed. "Sit and talk with me for a while."

Uncomfortable, she switched Rosie to the other breast to release the awful pressure in it, then sat next to him. Rosie lost interest a few minutes later and fell back asleep, but at least Briar didn't feel like her boobs were going to burst anymore.

She burped Rosie then set her in the bassinet by the couch. When she turned around Matt surprised her by stretching out on his back once more and pulling her on top of him. "You're a lot heavier than Rosie," he teased.

She settled over him, poked him in the ribs. "Hush."

A low chuckle rumbled through his chest, right under her cheek. "So," he asked, one hand gliding up and down her back in a soothing rhythm. "What happened?"

There was no point in avoiding this or pretending everything was fine, even if it made her feel ashamed. It was easier to talk about while not having to look him in the eye, though.

"It's the nights," she said after a pause. Confessing this was hard. "I don't know why. By lunchtime I usually feel pretty much normal, but for some reason when dinnertime rolls around and I start thinking about the night ahead, I feel...trapped. Lonely. Sad."

His hand never stopped stroking over her back. "Do you think you might have a touch of postpartum?"

What? "No. No, nothing as severe as that." Those women went through hell for months or years. She wasn't that bad, was she?

"Baby blues?"

"Maybe," she said grudgingly.

"It's pretty common. I read up on it last night."

Great. She'd had a meltdown and he'd felt the need to research to find out what the hell was wrong with her.

"A lot of the time it's due to hormone levels, and being constantly sleep deprived while recovering from a C-section makes it worse. I'm sorry for not realizing it was happening to you."

What? She squirmed inside. "It's not your fault. You help out when you can."

"You need to let me help more, and stop thinking you're supposed to do it all by yourself."

More guilt. Ugh. It was no secret she had a thing about being independent and in control, and that she had a problem with asking for help. "I feel like it's my job to look after her. I'm the mom. Every other mom seems to manage just fine."

"No, not even close. From what I read, almost eighty percent of new mothers go through it."

Briar lifted her head to look at him. "Really?"

He nodded, his expression serious. "I was surprised by how high it was too. I had no idea. The good news is, in most cases of baby blues things usually improve after a couple weeks. So if that's true, you should start to feel better soon."

She put her head back down. Huh. That made her feel a lot less of a freak. "I'm actually glad it's the baby blues. I thought there was something really wrong with me because I don't feel bonded to her the way I should be."

He kissed the top of her head. "Nope. Nothing wrong with you. You're a fantastic mother."

She snorted. "Yeah, fantastic. Look at me rocking the whole mom thing."

"Are you kidding? Look at Rosie. She's thriving, well

looked after, loved and protected. You're having a rough time right now and it's normal after all you've been through. But it's going to get better from here." He squeezed her tight. "I want you to stop being so hard on yourself. You're an amazing, attentive and loving mother. Rosie's a lucky little girl to have you taking care of her."

She huffed out a breath, his words hitting the squishiest, most insecure parts inside her that she didn't like to acknowledge. "You trying to make me freaking cry again, or what?"

Another chuckle. "No. But it's the truth."

"I hope she thinks shooting's cool, because I can barely cook. Just eggs."

"And cinnamon toast," he said with a smile in his voice.

"Yeah, that too." More comfortable now, feeling as though an invisible pressure valve inside her had been released, she lay there for a few minutes and savored the closeness. It was hard for her to ask because she didn't want to seem needy, but she craved affection from him right now more than ever. She'd needed this so much. "Just so we're clear, I don't want to see a counselor or talk to a doctor about this. And no meds. Not unless things get worse. Like I said, the nights are just tough for me right now. Once I start getting more sleep, I should be fine."

"I'm going to help more, so make peace with that. And if things still don't get better or even get worse, we're getting outside help," he said, his tone firm.

"Okay."

"All right, but then I'm gonna need you to let me help more, and promise to be honest with me."

She frowned. "I am honest with you."

"Not about this sort of thing. You've been trying to be superwoman since Rosie was born, and you haven't been honest about how you're feeling or what you need from me. You've been hiding that you're exhausted and overwhelmed and need a break." He sighed. "I don't know what it's going to take to get this through to you, but there's no shame in asking for help, especially from me. I *want* to help. We made Rosie together, didn't we? I hate it that you shut me out."

She'd hurt him. She'd never meant to do that. Hadn't even considered that her actions might. "You're right. I'm sorry."

He grunted in acknowledgment. "Now that we know what's going on we can deal with it together, and I promise to be more supportive and helpful."

He was right about all of it. She knew he was. Why was it still so damn hard for her to lean on the man she loved, or ask for help? "Okay."

"Yeah? You'll tell me when you're that tired, and speak up when you need a hand? Or a hug? Or sex, when we get to that again." He sighed. "God, I can't wait to get to that again."

She snickered at his half-kidding attempt to lighten the mood. "I'll try."

He tightened his grip. "Briar," he warned.

"Fine. I really will try." That was the best she could promise. She wasn't capable of transforming her entire personality overnight just because he wanted her to. But she absolutely needed to put some effort into making positive changes for their family's sake.

"Thank you." He was quiet a moment. "What about hiring a nanny part time?"

Briar shoved one hand into the couch and pushed up to scowl down at him, outraged. "Are you freaking insane? I'm not letting some stranger come in to look after my baby." Over her damn dead body that was happening. She would never trust an outsider to take care of Rosie at this age. Maybe ever. She'd cross that bridge when they got to it.

He grinned. "So protective. See? You're more bonded

to her than you seem to realize."

Briar considered that. Was she? She looked over at Rosie, asleep in the bassinet, and her lips curved into a tender smile. Yeah. Yeah, maybe she was.

The moment she thought it, it felt like a huge weight had been lifted from her shoulders. She loved Rosie. Would take on a freaking grizzly and kill it with her bare hands before ever letting it harm her child.

"I'm glad we had this talk," Matt teased.

"Me too." She leaned down to kiss his jaw, the corner of his mouth. "Now you'd better get up and shower if you want to get into work."

"I'll go in later to finish up some things." Pushing at her shoulders gently, they both sat up. "Then I'm taking some time off."

Her gaze snapped to his. "What? No."

He nodded. "As soon as I wrap up a couple things on my desk this afternoon I'm taking a leave of absence to help out more around here."

Oh, shit. "Matt, why did you do that? Now everyone will think I'm an incompetent loser—"

He held up a hand. "Stop. They don't know shit except that I want time at home with you and Rosie while she's little. And don't talk about yourself that way."

She glowered at him. "For how long?"

"Three months."

"That long?"

"It's not that long. And I'm not irreplaceable at work. I damn near missed Rosie's birth because I wasn't where I belonged—with you." He paused a beat, looking into her eyes. "When it counts, you and Rosie come first. My guys can survive without me. The world won't go to shit if I'm not involved with the teams. Other people are just as trained and capable as me at making critical decisions."

"Nobody's as good as you and you know it."

One side of his mouth curved up. "Well, thank you for

that."

It was the truth. "If you're doing this because you want more time with Rosie while she's small, then I'm okay with it. But if you're doing it because you're worried I can't handle it without you here, then—"

He put his fingers over her mouth to stop her. "I know you can handle it. But we're both at fault for what's happened with you. Me for assuming you were handling everything fine, and you for letting me think it. That's on both of us, and we both need to make changes." He paused, his expression softening. "This time is going to fly by, and I'm never getting it back. I want to be here. It'll make us all happier."

She eyed him, still doubtful.

"I'll still act as a consultant when necessary. Take calls, meetings maybe, things like that. But no travel, no long days or crazy schedules." He raised his eyebrows, daring her to argue with him. "You and I are a team. We're going to do this together from now on."

Well hell, she couldn't fault his arguments, and she sure wasn't going to say no to that last part. "All right. I'm on board with that."

He smiled. A slow, sexy smile that made her heart beat faster. "Good." He snagged her hand, pulled her off the couch. "Now let's go up and have a long shower together before Rosie wakes up. I know you love it when I wash your hair, massage your scalp and...other parts." He gave her a heated look that said that while they might not be able to have sex yet, they could still do plenty of other things in the meantime.

Okay, she wasn't going to say no to that either.

Epilogue

Five weeks later

Briar's eyes sprang open when Rosie's cry woke her from a deep sleep. She sat up, pushed to her feet, feeling light years better than she had during those first few weeks. Matt had taken the night shift to allow her a full night's sleep.

God, she missed sleep.

Having him around had been such a huge help. They worked well as a team, and the few times he had to act as a consultant for something work related, she was able to handle everything okay on her own. The awful sense of isolation and being overwhelmed had thankfully faded away with the mood swings about a month ago. She honestly didn't know how women with full-blown postpartum coped. It must be hell.

The worst bit now was the continual sleep deprivation, but with Rosie eating more and keeping most of it down, the amount of sleep they got was slowly improving too. That alone helped a ton.

She walked down the hallway, the wood floors cool

against her bare feet, and pushed the nursery door open. "Good morning," she said to Rosie.

The baby's head turned toward her, and Rosie's little face transformed into a look of pure delight, her lips curving as they parted. Briar stopped dead. "Did you just smile at me?"

Rosie did it again.

Oh my God. Briar reached into the crib and scooped her up, whirled and rushed back down the hall. "Matt! Matt, you gotta see this!"

"What?" he blurted, jerking up onto one elbow in the bed, the sheet falling down to reveal his naked, muscular torso. His eyes were bloodshot, his hair sticking up all over the place, and he was still the sexiest man she'd ever seen. "What's wrong?"

"Nothing." She looked down at Rosie proudly. "She just smiled at me."

A startled look came over his face. "She did?"

"She absolutely did." She looked down at their daughter. "Come on, Rosie. Do it again." She made a silly face, widening her eyes and opened her mouth in an exaggerated expression of excitement. "Come on, show your dad how clever you are."

Rosie stared up at her for a moment with eyes lightening to a shade of what looked like might end up being green, then looked around the room. No smile for daddy.

"She was totally smiling. I saw it *twice*," Briar said to Matt.

"I'll take your word for it." He chuckled, reached for the baby and drew her to his chest. "You're gonna make me work for my first smile, huh? Just when I think you can't get any smarter or more adorable."

"I think she's advanced. Most babies her age don't smile for another week or two."

Matt gave her a sardonic look. "Well of course she's

advanced. She's half Valkyrie, after all."

"True." Briar took Rosie back, waved a hand at him. The whole show and tell thing hadn't gone according to plan. "Go on back to sleep. I'm going to feed her and give her a bath." She shut the bedroom door behind her to let him sleep and headed downstairs. Rosie loved her baths but it was way easier in the stationary tub in the laundry room than in one of the bathtubs.

She reached the main level. Sunlight spilled through the kitchen windows, slanting across the wood floors in long rectangles. Briar settled on the couch to change and feed Rosie. Breastfeeding had gotten so much easier than it had been in the beginning. Her breasts weren't tender anymore, and she no longer had to bite her lip and brace herself when Rosie latched on. Her daughter was also draining one side completely at each feeding now, and almost always kept it all down.

After Rosie had finished feeding, Briar gave her a bath and put her in the little camo-print dress from Trinity, who was coming over tonight for dinner. "What do you think, little miss? Should we make your daddy some breakfast maybe? Take it upstairs to him? Not that we want him to get used to that sort of thing," she added. "Don't want to spoil him too badly, do we?"

She settled Rosie in her bouncy seat on the kitchen counter and puttered around making her and Matt something to eat, along with a pot of coffee. She was just gathering everything up to put it on a tray when she heard him coming down the stairs.

"What are you two up to in here?" he asked as he walked into the kitchen.

"We made you breakfast," Briar said. "But it was supposed to be breakfast in *bed*."

Matt's eyes gleamed. "Really? Were you going to hand feed it to me too?"

"Yeah, don't push it." She slid the tray across the

island toward him.

A gorgeous grin broke out over his handsome face. "Scrambled eggs and cinnamon toast. My favorites."

"They'd better be," Briar said with a grin, handing him a mug of coffee.

Matt turned to the baby. "What do you think, Miss Rosie? Are they my favorites?"

She slapped her clumsy hands on the bouncy chair, gave another smile.

Briar whipped out an arm to point at her. "There! You saw it, right? Tell me you saw it."

"That is the cutest damn thing I've ever *seen*," Matt gushed, scooping Rosie up to cover her face and neck with kisses. In another few weeks, the house would be filled with the sound of baby giggles. Briar couldn't wait to hear them.

Grinning, she leaned against the counter with her own mug of coffee and watched Matt lavishing affection on their daughter. It was unreal. She loved the two of them more than she'd ever believed herself capable of. Things had gotten off to a shaky start in the beginning, but now she knew they were going to be okay.

They were a family. She may be a long way from a perfect mother by some people's standards, but Rosie would grow up in a secure home knowing every day that she was loved by both her parents. Wasn't that the best any parent could do?

And if some asshole *ever* dared to hurt her baby girl, Briar would hunt the bastard down herself, kill him, then dispose of the body in a way that no one would ever find it.

She might even let Matt help a little.

—The End—

Dear reader,

Thank you for reading Guarded. I hope you enjoyed it. If you'd like to stay in touch with me and be the first to learn about new releases you can:

Join my newsletter at:
http://kayleacross.com/v2/newsletter/

Find me on Facebook:
https://www.facebook.com/KayleaCrossAuthor/

Follow me on Twitter:
https://twitter.com/kayleacross

Follow me on Instagram:
https://www.instagram.com/kaylea_cross_author/

Also, please consider leaving a review at your favorite online book retailer. It helps other readers discover new books.

Happy reading,
Kaylea

Excerpt from

Fractured Honor

Crimson Point Series

By Kaylea Cross

Copyright © 2018 Kaylea Cross

Chapter One

"I've got movement, eighty yards northeast of target. One male, two bodyguards exiting a silver Toyota pickup," Captain Beckett Hollister murmured into his mic. Lying prone behind some scrub brush on a ridge overlooking the target below, he had a perfect view of the building through his high-powered binos.

A mud-colored brick compound Beckett's twelve man SF A-Team had been sent out last night to provide recon on, now slowly lightening on its eastern side as the first weak rays of sunlight peeked over the Anti-Lebanon Mountains. They'd been waiting up here since oh-dark-hundred, providing intel to command back at headquarters outside of Damascus. The mission was fluid, could change at any time from a simple recon job into a direct assault on the position, or providing backup for the Delta unit currently on standby to perform the arrest and rescue.

"Copy that," headquarters responded. "Can you get a visual ID on any of them?"

Without lowering the binos, Beckett spoke in a low voice to Jase Weaver, his assistant operations and intel sergeant, stretched out beside him. "Recognize him?"

143

Weaver was quiet a few moments while he did his own assessment. "Negative."

Whoever the newcomer was, he wasn't their high value target, or even on the list of suspects they'd been given at the mission briefing. Which meant the three American security contractors being held hostage down there by the wanted militant leader were going to have to wait a while longer for rescue. Command wanted Delta to perform the assault and rescue, not Beckett's team, and only when the militant leader was present. A one-and-done op.

Beckett had been through and seen a lot over his twenty years of service to his country, but this kind of situation never got any less infuriating. Fucked up as it might be, at the end of the day, capturing this HVT was worth more to the American government than saving its imprisoned citizens—who had been sent here on its dime in the first place to guard some of its officials.

Beckett and his team didn't give a shit about the politics behind it; they were here to do their job. But no matter what command said, it was impossible to disregard their three countrymen being held down there. They had read the files on the captives. Knew their names and faces, where they came from. Two of them were Army vets, men who had served their country faithfully. Beckett wanted to help get them out.

Except all he could do right now was wait.

He remained silent with the rest of his twelve-man team spread around him in two groups as the minutes ticked slowly by, until more than an hour had passed. Lowering the binos, he cupped his gloved hands and blew on his frozen fingers to thaw them. At this elevation and time of year, this part of Syria was damn cold. His nose and lips had gone numb hours ago, and he could barely feel his toes even with the thick winter socks and heavy boots.

"Damn, it's as cold here as it was back in Afghanistan," Weaver said in a low voice.

"I hadn't noticed."

"That's because you're freaking *old*. Most of your nerve endings are probably already dead."

Beckett cracked a smile. "I wish." At thirty-nine, he was the oldest on the team and his body definitely felt all the aches and pains that came with two decades of punishing military service. A little less feeling in some areas would be welcome right now, especially in his troublesome lower back that felt seventy most days.

"Well, give it another couple hours and it'll be just above freezing again. We can pretend we're in the mountains in California instead of here."

"By all means, pretend away." Special Forces life wasn't easy. Now that he only had a few more months left in his contract, Beckett was seriously considering getting out this time. The army had given him a lot but his service had already cost him several nagging injuries, more dead friends than any man should ever lose, and his marriage. He wanted the chance to enjoy what was left of his life.

Or at least try to.

He reached into his front pocket for the last of his MRE, now a frozen lump in its package. Tasted like hell but it was protein and calories that would keep his core temp steady, so he couldn't complain. And as soon as they completed this mission, there was a hot shower and a pot of coffee waiting for him back at base. He didn't even care if it was stale, as long as it was hot and black.

"I'm guessing you don't feel like sharing that."

Beckett glanced at Weaver. "Not really."

"Dickwaffle."

"That's Captain Dickwaffle, to you." He made a low grumbling sound of appreciation as he chewed the next bite, earning a chuckle from his teammate that cut off sharply a split-second later.

"They're moving the prisoners," Weaver said.

Beckett snatched up his binos and took a look. Sure enough, armed guards were herding the prisoners from the building into an open courtyard in the center of the compound. One guard for each of them.

He informed command, his mind already racing ahead. Moving the prisoners out into an exposed position where they could be seen only made sense if the captors intended to put on a show and make a statement to anyone watching. And they had to know the American government had people watching. Right now Beckett and his team were the only unit close enough to offer some kind of response and make a rescue attempt if things went south.

"Hey, Cap. Seven o'clock off the courtyard."

At another teammate's words, Beckett focused there, his heart jolting when he saw the man who emerged from the shadows to stand at the edge of the courtyard. "You guys all seeing this?" Spread out as they were at various points along the ridge, everyone had a different vantage point and angle.

"Affirm," Weaver and another one of his guys said at the same time.

"Snipers, what's your status?" Beckett asked.

"Alpha and Bravo teams both green at this time."

Beckett informed command. "Be advised, a secondary HVT is on scene." He gave the man's name. Someone affiliated to the HVT the government was desperate to capture in this op. "Looks like he's inspecting the hostages. Both sniper teams are green."

"Copy that, team leader. Hold your positions."

"Roger. Is the assault force en route?" Command had been annoyingly silent about the Delta team's positioning. If they were going to do the captives any good, they'd better be damn close.

"We're alerting them now."

Translation: the Delta boys weren't getting here anytime soon, and likely wouldn't even be launched unless the primary HVT showed up.

He shelved the curse in his head. "Understood. Request permission to move in for—"

"Negative. Hold your position."

Beckett clenched his jaw and didn't respond. He was trained to be calm under pressure, in any given situation. To maintain a clear head and make decisions, sometimes hard ones, in bad circumstances. Even in a firefight his heart didn't elevate much. But being so close with this asshole right out in the open and in their sights, and not being able to act while three American lives were on the line tested his resolve.

Beckett watched the newcomer position himself in the middle of the courtyard to study the prisoners. All blindfolded, hands bound behind them. Beckett wanted to get in there, capture the secondary HVT and save the hostages while they had the chance. Not wait to see if the primary HVT would magically appear in time so they could act.

"Oh, shit, Cap…"

He tensed at Weaver's low voice and shifted his gaze right. Down in the courtyard, a struggle had broken out. One of the hostages must have reached his limit because he was now fighting back against his captor.

Cole Goodman. An army vet-turned-contractor from Ohio.

The two men rolled on the ground for a moment before the captor came up on top, straddling his bound and blindfolded prisoner. He landed several brutal punches to the helpless man's face while the militants swarmed around the prisoners like angry bees.

Beckett and his team were too far away to hear what was being said, even with the parabolic listening dish, but it was clear that things had just taken a deadly turn.

He informed command of what was happening, then spoke to his sniper teams again. Both responded that they were green. One command from him, and they could help even the odds down there.

They had maybe seconds to do something to prevent the worst. Take out the armed men and the bodyguards, maybe stop what he knew was coming. "Sir, request permission to—"

"Negative."

He took a breath, tried again. "Sir. We need to act *now* if we're going to save those men."

"Captain, you will maintain your position and await further orders," the man said in a hard tone.

It took everything Beckett had to keep his tone professional. "Understood." He shared a hard look with Weaver, the frustration eating him alive as he went back to watching what was going on in the courtyard. Only the self-control drilled into him and the desire to avoid seeing his guys wind up facing court-martials and dishonorable discharges for disobeying orders kept him from giving the command to open fire on the tangos.

"They're gonna kill them," Weaver said.

Beckett didn't answer. With orders and rules of engagement preventing his team from doing a goddamn thing other than watch, they were forced to hold in position and let the inevitable unfold.

He stared through his binos with a sinking heart as Goodman was seized by the hair and dragged to his knees. Blood covered his face. He struggled weakly but the beating had depleted his strength and even without that he had no chance.

The other two captives were forced to their knees beside him. One of them bowed his head. His mouth twisted, shoulders jerking as he faced the certainty of his death.

Beckett's heart drummed in his ears. "They're about to execute the hostages," he warned command. *For fuck sake, let us do something. It's not too late to stop this.* But it would be in another few seconds.

It took a moment for the response to come back. "Understood. My original order still holds."

Cold spread through him. He forced himself to lie still, called on all his discipline as he watched the armed militants gather into a line in front of the hostages. Three men stepped forward, raising their weapons.

Around him, Beckett's entire team was silent. All of them having front row seats to watch the doomed men. It took everything he had not to close his eyes or look away.

The militants opened fire.

The AKs' reports echoed sharp across the valley floor and up the side of the ridge to Beckett and his team. Down in the courtyard, all three hostages lay sprawled dead in the dust, their hands still bound behind them.

He took a deep breath. "All three hostages down," he reported quietly, his tone flat even as anger seethed inside him.

"Copy that."

A wave of rage pulsed through him. This. *This* was the shit that ate through a man's soul and haunted him the rest of his life.

He drew another quiet breath. *I'm done.* The thought was loud and clear in his head. "Snipers, what's your status now?" he asked, though he already knew the answer because the HVT had just stepped back inside the building.

"Alpha and Bravo both red at this time."

They'd not only sat by doing nothing while the hostages were executed, they'd also missed the window to take out the secondary HVT. Now that asshole was safely barricaded back inside the compound, laughing at them while the American contractors lay dead in the courtyard.

Those men hadn't had to die. God*damn* it.

"Captain, return to base with your team. Intel suggests the primary HVT is headed to a different location."

"Roger that." It was a relief to lower the binos. But even though he no longer had to stare at the dead men his team could have saved, he would still see their faces for a long time whenever he closed his eyes. "Come on, boys. Let's go." He eased backward down the rear side of the ridge before standing and shouldering his ruck, welcoming the stab of pain in his lower back that shot down the rear of both legs. The shadows were deeper here, the cold penetrating bone deep.

It didn't match the ice in the center of his chest.

Next to him, Weaver didn't say anything, his jaw set, anger and frustration burning in his aqua gaze. Beckett understood. He was done with this shit.

The heavy, sick feeling that condensed in the pit of his belly as they humped back down the ridge for extraction solidified his decision. He was so damn tired of the wasted lives, of the weight he carried on his conscience.

It was time for him to get out and go home. And not simply stateside to North Carolina.

Home.

To Crimson Point, Oregon. The only place outside of the army where he'd ever truly felt like he belonged.

Fractured Honor will release in September 2018!

About the Author

NY Times and USA Today Bestselling author Kaylea Cross writes edge-of-your-seat military romantic suspense. Her work has won many awards, including the Daphne du Maurier Award of Excellence, and has been nominated multiple times for the National Readers' Choice Awards. A Registered Massage Therapist by trade, Kaylea is also an avid gardener, artist, Civil War buff, Special Ops aficionado, belly dance enthusiast and former nationally-carded softball pitcher. She lives in Vancouver, BC with her husband and family.

You can visit Kaylea at www.kayleacross.com. If you would like to be notified of future releases, please join her newslette: http://kayleacross.com/v2/newsletter/

Complete Booklist

ROMANTIC SUSPENSE

DEA FAST Series
Falling Fast
Fast Kill
Stand Fast
Strike Fast
Fast Fury
Fast Justice
Fast Vengeance

Colebrook Siblings Trilogy
Brody's Vow
Wyatt's Stand
Easton's Claim

Hostage Rescue Team Series
Marked
Targeted
Hunted
Disavowed
Avenged
Exposed
Seized
Wanted
Betrayed
Reclaimed
Shattered
Guarded

Titanium Security Series
Ignited
Singed

Burned
Extinguished
Rekindled
Blindsided: A Titanium Christmas novella

Bagram Special Ops Series
Deadly Descent
Tactical Strike
Lethal Pursuit
Danger Close
Collateral Damage
Never Surrender (a MacKenzie Family novella)

Suspense Series
Out of Her League
Cover of Darkness
No Turning Back
Relentless
Absolution

PARANORMAL ROMANCE
Empowered Series
Darkest Caress

HISTORICAL ROMANCE
The Vacant Chair

EROTIC ROMANCE (writing as *Callie Croix*)
Deacon's Touch
Dillon's Claim
No Holds Barred
Touch Me
Let Me In
Covert Seduction

35311219R00095

Printed in Great Britain
by Amazon